The Saga of Krait Hall

Birke Duncan

Copyright © 2014 by Birke Duncan, M.A.

Send all correspondence to: Northwest Folklore, Dept. of Scandinavian Studies, University of Washington, Box 353420, Seattle, WA 98195-3420

First edition, first printing

Printed in the United States of America

Printed by Gorham Printing, Centralia, Washington

TABLE OF CONTENTS

The Hanger-On Drops In 1

Monty Moudlyn 41

Lesson Plan 53

Roscoe Gat 69

A Janitor's Territory 85

My Script Is M*U*D 91

Bob's Progress 101

Independent Study 107

The Saga of Krait Hall 123

Afterword 149

The Hanger-On Drops In

I

January & February are pointless in the Bruce Department Store. Few customers come in. The lowest floor, the men's department, becomes cavernous and eerily quiet.

Not today.

Rolly Harris, newly hired piano player, and boyfriend of a salesgirl, took his amateur tightrope walking act to the fourth floor. He shouted joyfully, "Follow your bliss. Whoo!" But joy turned into a howl of terror, followed by a muffled thud.

His girlfriend, Chelsea McGuffin, screamed from the top floor.

Sportswear manager Miles Roomer dashed to the center our department, then ran back and forth. He shouted, "I saw it! He fell!"

I walked in, joining Miles and my old flame, Molly Daniels. She questioned Miles, "Who fell?"

"Chelsea McGuffin's boyfriend."

"Rolly?"

"Yes, Rolly. I think he's dead."

"No, he can't be."

"I've got to check the manual for how to deal with this."

Miles fled toward the back room. Apparently, it never occurred to him to call an ambulance. I sidled calmly to the telephone, and asked Molly, "Was Rolly trying to fly?"

Molly did a double-take, "Jim, how did you get back to this sales floor so fast? I thought you took the escalator upstairs after Rolly & Chelsea."

She was correct to suspect me, but I stayed calm and cool on the phone: I told the 911 operator to send an aid car to the Bruce Department Store on Fifth Avenue in Seattle.

No, I explained, Rolly had not fallen outdoors. We have an atrium effect inside.

He plays the piano on the second floor, four hours per day.

No, I had not checked his vitals. He had landed on a large, open cardboard box, so I couldn't see him directly. All I had seen was his left arm, dangling limply over the side of the container.

My name? James Western.

I waited until the dispatcher hung up, then replaced the receiver. I had done my duty.

Molly stood at the sales counter right next to me. Her fierce glare reminded me of when we had broken up, twenty-one years earlier.

"Well," I observed, "It looks like my efforts to break up that little romance are a moot point."

"You don't seem too upset, Jim.

"It's all part of life's grand scheme."

She folded her arms and asked, "How did he fall?"

"Carelessness plus gravity."

"Don't be flippant. I wouldn't put anything past you."

I commented, rather than asked, "You suspect homicide."

She nodded.

"Well, in that case, find our antsy colleague, Byron Davenport. He seethed with envy on many levels."

Molly tightened her folded arms. I had hoped to distract her, but that didn't work. "Let's try this again, Jim. You came back to work at this store four weeks ago. You convinced everyone but me that you were here for research on a book."

"Right."

"You've never had a straightforward agenda in your life. Admit the truth."

"I was downstairs on this floor, when Rolly took a tumble. It was like file footage of those acrobats, the Flying Wallendas."

Meanwhile, a crowd of workers and a few female customers had come down the escalator, and gathered around the box where Rolly lay. Distant sirens grew louder, drowning out the onlookers' murmurs and coughs.

Molly maintained an icy stare.

"Don't you believe me?" I asked.

She shook her head.

You can't convince someone of anything, once they've lost all regard for you.

II

That was how my plans came together. The sordid tale begins decades earlier, but we won't get into it here.

Instead, I'll begin with my return to the Bruce Department Store. I came in two weeks after the Christmas rush, with written permission from the desk of Norton Bruce himself, which I presented to Miles Roomer.

The skinny young man shook my hand and welcomed me aboard, at a desk obscured by rows of shelving for folded jeans and shirts. He accompanied me through this maze, onto the sales floor, then called out to the skeleton crew, "It's meeting time."

The three of them groaned. They were my lost love, Molly; a small, much younger lady; and a young man in an immaculate suit. They set down the heavy khaki pants and merino wool sweaters they had been folding; then the trio dragged their feet over to us. Molly's jaw tightened when our eyes met.

"This is Jim Western," said Miles, "He's kind of a seasonal worker. Jim wrote his Master's thesis in organizational psychology on the Bruce Department Store. Now he's returned for more research, or something like that. He can also make sales, and doesn't need training."

I added, "Thank you, Miles. This is basically a work-study immersion project. It's nice to meet all of you, except Molly."

The younger sales people and Miles all looked directly at her. I explained, "We know each other a little too well."

Miles introduced me to my new co-workers, Chelsea McGuffin, whom I had seen before; and Byron Davenport.

The manager switched gears, "Now that we're acquainted, we come to the second part of the meeting. All of our sales have been down, especially Byron."

He nodded toward the pale, twitchy man in the gray pinstripe suit.

Miles didn't look like a manager. Too young, too strangely dressed in purple corduroys and a green, cashmere sweater. Static from the latter made individual hair strands stick up on his curly blond head.

Byron, however, had carefully coiffed brown hair with a razor sharp part on the right side. But on closer inspection, the pallor of Byron's face emphasized dark circles around red-tinged eyes. He looked sideways at Miles: "Of course my sales are down," he said in crisply enunciated tones, "It's mid-January. The customers blew their money on Christmas shopping." He pointed to a rack of hangers and a row of shelves, "We just had the biggest snowstorm in recent years, yet we're supposed to sell swimming suits and polo shirts. Customers ask me for sweaters and coats."

"Wrong," countered Miles, "Your sales have dropped because you have not been engaging clients outside of the store. This obviously isn't the job for you. Even so, I don't want you to imagine that I'm singling you out."

Miles had said this to the very person he singled out. Then our manager made eye contact with me, "Everyone here needs a pep talk. When the customer enters, you become his best friend. Show the client every product that matches his lifestyle. He'll trust you to the point where he buys it all. The next day, call the customer at home. Ask him how the purchases work for him. After that, send him notes. Call him at work and at home. Tell him what's on sale. Don't let him forget you. The clothes belong to the customer, but the customer belongs to you. Good luck, and good selling." Miles turned and walked away.

Molly patted Byron on the shoulder, "You heard Miles, we need to engage the customers."

"More like enrage the customers. Do I stop if they file a restraining order?"

"Let me give you some advice. Ignore Miles. Everyone else does. Besides, it's not so bad here, Byron. Just be glad you don't sell cars. You'd have to live entirely on commission. Imagine how you would feel when those customers walked out on you."

"At least I could run them over with the merchandise."

He sulked back to folding sweaters and pants.

"That's the spirit." Molly addressed me directly, through gritted teeth: "Welcome back, Jim."

She said that with all the warmth of an Arctic blizzard.

"Molly, my dear," I said, "Are you still mad at me about that chapter on you in my thesis?"

"You know it goes back farther than that."

"My mother said I should get a girlfriend who had a lot in common with me."

"We still broke up, we just run into each other more often. What's with the phony reason for being here? You have a doctorate and you're on the UW faculty."

"Publish or perish. I'm incognito and on sabbatical."

"For how long, nine months?"

That stung, but I maintained my geniality, "Not likely. I'm more careful these days. And so are the women."

"But why would you leave in the middle of the academic year? I'll bet you seduced an undergraduate."

"Just one? Give me more credit than that, Molly. Nubile females lust after the sophisticated older gentleman, especially when their grades improve. Do you know that I'm better looking now than I was twenty years ago?"

"That won't work on me. I was there, remember? Were you planning to prey on the women here?"

"Maybe I'll ignite an old flame."

"Not this one."

"Extend the metaphor, Molly. Why not admit you're carrying a torch for me?"

"Do you think you're funny? I'm not playing your games, Jim."

A conversation started behind us, at the table where Byron and Chelsea folded a pile of pants.

Molly had bested me in a battle of wits, and I had fallen flat. I said to her, "Well, I'm also interested in interpersonal fireworks, like that."

I flourished my hand in the direction of the young pair.

Byron said to Chelsea, "Customers are pikers. I hate this job."

I finally got to hear Chelsea speak. She had a scratchy voice, like a mewing kitten: "*Caveat emptor.*" I found out the translation later: "Let the buyer beware."

Byron replied, "*Carthago delenda est.*" (Carthage must be destroyed.)

Chelsea patted Byron's arm and assured him, "*Illegitimati non carborundum.*" (Don't let the bastards grind you down.)

I turned to Holly and asked, "What exactly is Byron's problem?"

"He's a whole other chapter for you. Byron Davenport has salesman's burnout."

"Do you mean like teacher burnout?"

"I suppose. He earned a Master's degree in some useless liberal arts field, and this was the highest paying job he could get. Byron hates customers, hates the products, hates the training, and hates the manager."

"How do you know all this?"

"Byron joins me for lunch sometimes in the cafeteria."

"That must be uplifting. What keeps him here?"

I didn't receive an answer to that question, because a new figure entered. This formed my first impression of Rolly Harris. He was well over 30 years old, though he had two-toned brown and orange hair, with an annoying soul-patch on his chin.

The tall, thin man said, "Hi, everybody." Then he strutted over to Chelsea, a blonde a foot shorter than him, and bent down to kiss her lips.

Molly said, "Chelsea, no public displays of affection are allowed. You know that."

"Sorry, Mom," said Chelsea.

Molly's shoulders jolted, but she resumed her school-marm composure: "Don't call me that. I'm not even forty yet."

Molly retreated. I whispered to my former beloved, "Does she know something?"

"No."

Chelsea held Rolly's hand and gazed up into his eyes. like an astronomer at a comet.

Byron stopped folding and said without smiling, "Ah, yes, it's Rolly Harris; he who walks in the Shoes of the Fisherman."

Rolly must have missed the allusion, because he said, "I've already been a fisherman."

"Unemployed now," announced Byron.

"I spent a summer fishing in Alaska. It was the highest paying job I've ever had."

Molly smiled and said, "It's probably the only job you've ever had."

I pried, "Hi, Rolly, I'm Jim Western. How have you made a living?"

"Playing my git-box on the street and cafes, writing songs for stage shows, musical director of plays at three different high schools." He stroked Chelsea's shoulder and said, "It's time to play catch-up with this little love kitten."

Byron winced. "He's out of work, yet he has a girlfriend. Women treat me like a bum for having a job."

Not wanting to hear Byron's complaints, I pulled Molly aside and confided, "I recognized Chelsea from last November, on a Christmas shopping foray. I bought a parting gift for one of my co-eds. A wool scarf."

"Not even a pewter pin? You're a regular Sir Galahad." She called past me, "Chelsea, it's time you met Jim Western."

Chelsea walked over and asked, "Am I going to be in the research for your book about the workplace?"

"I guarantee it."

Rolly followed after her, "How about me?"

"Your name might come up," I told him, "under workplace distractions."

"I always wanted to be in a book," said Rolly. Then he kissed Chelsea obnoxiously. He bade her a poetic adieu: "Later."

She didn't just smile when he departed, her eyes took on a dreamy cast.

III

As days progressed, I found time to get to know Chelsea. Here's an example. We were both scrubbing a counter covered with fingerprints, by spraying it with rubbing alcohol and then wiping it with rags.

I asked, "So, Chelsea, do you plan to make a career of the Bruce Store?"

"I was planning on medical school," she explained. My heart jumped. "I took four years of Latin in high school, plus every biology, chemistry, and math class in community college. I'm taking a break now."

"Medical school is the best possible goal. You're twenty years old, so you've got time."

She stopped scrubbing and asked, "How did you know my age?"

"Molly mentioned it. You're better than this department store. You have more potential here than anyone else."

Byron walked over with a load of unfolded shirts and slacks. He must have overheard, because he joined in the conversation, uninvited, "Thanks for rubbing it in, Jim. She may have potential, but she still goes out with that pretentious Rolly Harris. *Degustibus non est disputantandum.*"

"What was that?" I asked.

Chelsea translated: "There's no accounting for taste."

Byron added, "*Tempus fuget. Disce pati.*"

"Time flies. Learn to suffer."

I nodded thoughtfully. A deeper conversation became impossible with Byron hanging around.

I walked over to Molly. She had planted herself by the base of the escalator, in hopes of catching a customer on the way down to our floor. I pointed to Chelsea and Byron folding clothes at the cash register.

I observed, "If Byron is the competition, no wonder she chose Rolly."

"The saleswomen from other floors and I have told her to dump Rolly. That just drives her closer to him. We finally agreed it was none of our business."

"How original. Look, Molly, I hate to see Chelsea's brilliant mind wasted in intellectually mediocre surroundings."

"Thanks for the compliment, Jim."

"Present company excepted, of course. Think of that girl's DNA. It's like she's a product of eugenics. You leave Rolly to me."

"Stay out of this."

"Rolly Harris is not the only bad influence."

"Right, one just came to work here recently."

"No, I mean Byron." I nodded my head in his direction. Byron rocked back and forth, muttering to himself. "How does he make any sales? He has the disposition of a troll."

Organizational psychology made me genuinely curious about the group dynamics of these co-workers. Miles emerged from the back room and ambushed Byron.

"Byron, you need to work on your customer approach," Miles pulled out a card and read aloud: "Smile at the customer, give an open body hello, and always have a product in hand." Miles put the card away, and asked, "How many thank you cards have you sent to customers this week?"

"Fourteen."

"Well, it's a start. You need to send them all the time."

The phone rang in the background, so Molly rushed over and picked it up.

Miles Roomer's lecture continued, "Customers wait around, hoping for positive attention. They need to know that we care. Then they'll avoid all other department stores, because they'll feel wanted and needed here. When a customer shops at our store, they are ours for life."

"What do you do?" snarled Byron, "Memorize manager's clichés?"

I would have fired him for that, but Molly called out, "Byron? It's for you. Mr. Jackson said he got one of your notes."

Byron squared his shoulders and marched to the phone with the first sign of confidence I'd seen from him.

But during Byron's short conversation, his back hunched and his head hung further downward. I heard him assure the customer that he was following the store's policy, he was sorry, and he would inform his manager.

Byron returned the phone to the cradle.

Miles walked over and instructed, "You should always say good-bye."

"He had already hung up."

"It's good to answer the phone. You'll get a sale without any effort."

"Let me know when that happens. Mr. Jackson said that my note to them about a sale was presumptuous, since he and his wife like to shop around. He told me never to contact them again."

Even if Miles heard Byron's account, it still didn't dissuade him from parroting the company line: "Byron, you need to think of serving a customer like going on a first date. You're getting to know each other. And you always call that person the next morning."

The mind boggled at the number of ways to ridicule that advice. Byron said, "I made fun of that analogy several months ago in the training seminar."

Miles said, "I wasn't the trainer."

"No, but you're repeating her speech, word-for-word."

"Just remember what I said." Miles replied. Byron went back to folding shirts.

I whispered to Molly, "You're right, you little spitfire. Byron's burnout could become a whole new chapter. You know how to help me, even after all these years. Don't you want to rekindle our romance?"

"What do you do," asked Molly, "sit around thinking up fire metaphors?"

"No second chance for me? What are you going to do, take up with Rolly?"

"Rolly and Molly? I don't think so. Rolly is over thirty years old, but he acts like someone in his early 20s.

"I was like Rolly once, and look how I turned out."

"Vain?"

"No banter, please. You know how I used to be."

Byron and Miles walked over to us. For once, they were the curious observers.

Miles said, "No, how were you, Jim?"

I could never resist becoming the center of attention. "I was the cliché of the party animal. I discovered how to blow my studies, chase girls, and booze it up all weekend long."

Molly said, "He planned to major in hedonism at The Evergreen State College."

"It all caught up with me pretty fast," I continued, "I got a girl pregnant, and it changed our lives irrevocably. Let that be a lesson to all young men."

"You can't wrap it up neatly like a gift box," said Molly, "Did you marry the girl?"

"No."

"Did you support the baby?"

"No."

"Did you skip town?"

"Yes. My Dad called me a disgrace to the family. Both sets of parents decided we should put the baby up for adoption, and go to schools in different states. In fact her parents sent her for a year of study in Costa Rica."

"And what happened to the baby?" asked Molly.

I'm accustomed to amateur interrogators, so I continued with her game by answering truthfully. "The baby girl wound up in the nice home of a middle aged couple who couldn't have kids. They were friends of the Bruce family. I got my education at a disgusting, substandard diploma mill, with no real sense of education. Research didn't matter, just passion. Whoever yelled loudest won the debate."

"Where was that?" asked Miles.

"Stanford."

Molly asked, "What about the baby's mother?"

And again, I answered truthfully, "I still have feelings for her, and I'd like to think she feels the same way about me."

Molly shook her head and turned away.

IV

Several days passed, with a few customers now and again. Male customers blew past Byron, Miles, and me, in order to have Chelsea or Molly wait on them.

I spent a half hour helping a Brazilian look for jeans, and dug through the metal and press-board shelves in the back room, until I finally found two pairs in his size. By the time I came out, he had moved on to Chelsea. He eventually departed with three bags of merchandise. I smiled and nodded to him. He looked down, and wouldn't make eye contact with me.

Chelsea sashayed over waving a copy of the receipt like a flag. The Brazilian tourist had spent $1776.

I was proud of her.

Then one quiet, tedious Monday, a stocky, stooped old man shuffled in. He dressed casually, in a brown corduroy jacket, turtleneck, and wrinkled khaki pants. Most of his hair had thinned away, except for red and white strands on his pate, and short fringe around the side and back of his head.

But he also had a wry smile, and playful eyes, like a statue of Voltaire. I knew exactly who he was. Miles, Molly, Chelsea, Byron, and I formed a reviewing line.

Miles said, "Mr. Bruce, thank you so much for coming to see us. I'm sure you're here for a very important reason."

The sprightly old gent ignored Miles completely and beheld the lithe beauty with the mane of brown hair. Mr. Bruce looked Molly up and down, then said, "Hi-ya, cutie."

"Hello, sir," she replied, "It's always a pleasure."

"How old are you now, honey? Twenty-nine?"

"Thank you. I'm actually thirty-seven.

"Yes, I'd love to go out to dinner with you, a lady close to my own age." He punctuated that flirtation with a wink.

"I'll say," said Molly, "My age times two."

"Got a boyfriend?"

"Not lately," Her eyes shifted in my direction, then back to him, "I've had some bad experiences."

"I can change that. Young women like sophisticated older men."

"The more sophisticated, the better."

"And the older they are, the more sophisticated—and wealthier. We'll talk again later."

For once it was my turn to wince. How many old men could get away with that?

Mr. Bruce looked at Chelsea and said, "Hello, pretty girl. Chelsea isn't it?"

Chelsea confirmed her identity, and thanked Mr. Bruce for remembering.

He said, "I never forget a beautiful woman's face."

I didn't realize the significance of that statement until much later.

Mr. Bruce looked back to Molly and said, "Sorry, Miss Daniels, just trying to make you jealous."

Mr. Bruce stopped next at my male colleague. "Hello again. What was your name? Shelley?"

"Byron."

"Stock room?"

"That's a good idea," said Byron with energy, and not a trace of sarcasm, "I'm currently in sales. When can I start in back?"

"Oh, I don't make those decisions any more. It's up to your manager, Pretty Boy Miles Roomer."

Miles smiled proudly, raised his sharp chin, and puffed out his meager chest. Miles intoned, "Byron, you need to shine on the sales floor, and develop real rapport with the customers. That's when I'll let you work away from them, in the back room."

Mr. Bruce patted Miles on the back, "You're a great motivator, Miles."

Byron inserted, "Yes, sir. Every time I meet with him, I feel like jumping off a roof."

"Your satisfaction wouldn't last long, would it?" asked the wise old gentleman, "Believe me, you're a long time dead. Make the most of your life, Byron, even if it isn't here. Good luck."

Byron crinkled his forehead, and asked our patriarch, "Did you just fire me?"

"I told you, I don't make those decisions." He turned away from Byron.

Byron murmured to Chelsea, "Old men should be smothered at birth."

I didn't want Byron to get fired just yet, since he might serve a purpose later.

I stepped forward, stuck out my hand, and said to Mr. Bruce, "Hi, Pinky."

That stopped our overlord. Mr. Bruce said, "That was my nickname in college."

"Really?" asked Molly, "Why was that?"

"Because of my red hair, at the time." He ran his thick right hand over what remained of his locks. He looked at me again and said, "Why, Jimmy Western, I haven't seen you in years. When did you come back?"

"Two weeks ago."

"You look more like your father every day. What a little scamp you were, sneaking under the fitting room door and scaring that half-naked lady out of her wits."

Byron asked me, "And they rehired you?"

"I was thirteen."

Molly said, "I never heard that story. What caused your behavior? Hormones?"

"No, I was playing with my remote-controlled car. It was the 1980s. The car rolled under a fitting room door. I was just trying to retrieve it. How was I to know the lady was trying on a bra?"

Molly gave me a knowing smile: "I'd say you had a pretty good idea."

Mr. Bruce continued, "I wouldn't want to see him do that now. Jim's Dad and I were in college together. This young man worked here every summer when he was at Stanford, then for two years until he got into Grad. School, and for a little while after that. Well, I'll see you kids later."

He shuffled away. I looked right at Byron and said, "There's a reason he's in charge."

Our line broke up and we headed back to various folding and straightening chores. Miles pointed to a table with heaps of lamb's wool and merino sweaters and said, "Hey, Chelsea, do you want to retag all those sweaters?"

"No, I don't want to do it," she replied, "but I will."

Miles scuttled off while Chelsea was in mid-quip. I said, "That was a good comeback, Chelsea." I joined her in the dull chore of scanning old SKU numbers, then printing up new prices on blank tags, and clipping them onto the labels.

While we slogged through the boring task, I said, "You have a deeper understanding of language than most people your age. I hate the way they talk. Nothing is worse than the verb, 'to go' in place of 'to say.' It's hard to follow when someone says:

"I go, 'Where'd he go?'

"John goes, 'Away.'

"I'm like, 'No way.'

"He's all, 'Dude, I'm gone. Peace out.'"

Chelsea smiled. "That's fun. We think alike, Jim."

We continued the chore in a comfortable silence, while I basked in what she had just said to me. When we finished, she headed off to another task.

Molly sidled up to me and asked, "What are you up to with Chelsea?"

"Establishing rapport."

"Does she remind you of someone?"

"Yes, Molly; a nice girl who was a little younger at the time, making one of the same mistakes."

And just then, Rolly Harris entered. I hadn't seen him in a while, but my heart sank. He said, "Hi, everybody. Chelsea, I had another business meeting."

Molly observed, "It's amazing how many business meetings an unemployed man can have."

"I met with my director," Rolly continued, "We're going to write a rock opera, based on *The Creature from the Black Lagoon*."

We stopped working, and gathered around.

I would have expected Molly to be the first person to attack Rolly's dream, but instead it was Byron: "A 1950s horror show as a rock opera; it'll never work."

"Sure it will," said Rolly, still beaming, "I can include some songs I've written about the Amazon rain forest. The band will enter, dressed as natives wearing masks. They'll chant about their homeland:

> Black Lagoon, glowing moon,
> Black Lagoon, creature soon.
> Black Lagoon, fear of night,
> Black Lagoon, seek the light.

"Hare Krishnas can go on like that for hours."

My training from Graduate School kicked in at last: "Chanting is a form of mind control. That way your followers can't think of anything else, like, 'Why am I sitting here, conforming?' A cult doesn't want independent thinkers. By the way, Hare Krishnas worship the Hindu deity of carnal love."

"Carnal love?" Rolly echoed as a question.

Byron said, "Does he have to spell it out for you? S-E-hex."

The subject must have made Byron uncomfortable, because he wandered away from the group, but still within earshot.

Rolly congratulated himself: "And I applied to be the piano player upstairs. The interviewer says I'm a shoo-in. I should get the job in three days."

Byron muttered, "It gets worse."

Rolly said, "I'll compose the rock opera arias here."

"And then he'll sing them," said Byron to himself.

"And then I'll sing them, and accompany myself on the piano."

"Why doesn't a piano fall on him?"

"The company doesn't need to pay me royalties," explained Rolly, "just a salary. All I need is a backer. The director and I compiled a budget of just fifty thousand dollars, including the cast album."

I broke away and confronted Byron, who said, "I've got to stop this."

I pulled the nattily dressed detractor aside, behind a long clothes rack: "Byron, I couldn't help hearing you talk to yourself."

"Don't you know eavesdropping is rude?"

"Yes, Rolly might think the same thing."

"I don't want him to fleece Mr. Bruce."

"Just stay out of it. Try running your own life."

"There's no fun in that."

"No, but it's a challenge."

Byron didn't answer. He said, "I'd better take a break."

I looked around at the empty sales floor and asked, "From what?"

"I'll harass customers with more unwanted cards."

"Good man."

Byron skulked away.

I turned around and walked right into Molly.

"Jim, I'm actually grateful to you for a change. We could have spent the next hour dealing with a variety of pointless complications."

"I know. Byron Davenport needs psychological help. It's more than frustration, or even a personality disorder."

"It's amazing how we co-workers focus on each other when business dies down."

"I'll mention that in my research, Molly."

"Come on, Jim. You're here for some other reason."

"Do you think I'm planning a heist?"

"I could see Rolly trying that, but not you."

"He's a dreamer."

"Maybe that's why Chelsea loves him."

"And that's why Rolly is holding Chelsea back professionally."

"I told you to stay out of it, Jim."

Talking to her alone like this awakened old feelings in my heart. I stood

16

next to Molly, put my arm around her shoulder, and said, "I'll stay out of it, if you provide me with a different focus. Yourself."

Molly brushed my hand off her shoulder and patted me twice on the arm: "It didn't work before, Jim."

She walked away, with the grace of a gazelle. I admired her slim frame in a green dress.

V

Rolly landed the piano playing job. The management allowed him to play some lyrical, original tunes but would not let him sing. My eyes burned whenever I saw Chelsea sitting side by side with him at a lunch room table, with his hand on her knee.

One day, he came down to our floor when Chelsea was in the fitting room corridor, waiting on a rare February client.

I had just finished ringing up a customer, so I called out, "Rolly, could you come here, please?"

He ambled over and gave me a cheerful hello. I said, "I was just talking to Molly."

"Do you mean the lady who makes wisecracks about me?"

"That's a form of flirtation. She's hiding tender feelings for you."

"Really?"

"Cross my heart. And you know something? I think she's right. Your girlfriend goes back to school this summer. I've attended and taught at universities for many years, and I see this all the time. Relationships break up. Chelsea will fall for some jock on a football scholarship, and you'll be out of the picture. But Molly Daniels? Molly's looking for attention from a creative, musical genius."

"Cool."

"Don't get me wrong. Chelsea is a great girl, but Molly is wonderful woman."

"What else can you tell me about Molly?"

"Most men are crazy about Molly. You've taken the right approach by being happy, pursuing your art, and showing no romantic interest.

Furthermore, she has to compete with Chelsea. That sends Molly right up the wall."

"I hate to think of hurting Molly's feelings."

"That's hardly your fault. Take charge. Give her a big hug and a kiss. Women love boldness."

"I don't know about that. Chelsea loves me."

"Then think of Molly as your insurance policy, if things don't work out with Chelsea. Be generous with your affections.

Molly glided across the sales floor. Rolly and I both watched her. He said to me, "Thanks for the heads-up, Jim."

And then Rolly made his approach. My scheme looked successful. Rolly would two-time Chelsea, and I could break them up. Then Chelsea would forget all this lovey-dovey romance and go on to a great career.

Rolly said, "Excuse me, Molly."

"Do you want to make a purchase?

"Look, I know how you feel about me."

She folded her arms, "Oh, you do?

"Yes, and I'm flattered."

"Flattered?"

"You're an attractive woman, for your age. You can have any man, so don't waste your time on me. I'm already taken."

"Where did you get this idea?"

"I have to admit you've covered up your feelings pretty well. Sorry, Molly. I hope you'll understand." He walked back to me and said, "I hated to do that, Jim."

Then he headed up the escalator, and back to the piano.

Molly closed her fists and marched toward me, with the look of a lioness. I had no escape, so I smiled and shrugged with mock embarrassment.

"Jim! What possessed you?"

"I just wanted to test Rolly's loyalty to Chelsea. He passed with flying colors. Too bad."

Before she could yell at me, I lied, "I've got a customer in the fitting room."

I beat a hasty retreat, and gave a quick greeting to none other than Mr. Bruce. He gave me a slap on the back then made a beeline for Molly. The shuffle was gone. A long-absent spring had returned to his step.

Mr. Bruce maneuvered behind Molly and massaged her shoulders. "I can't stand seeing a beautiful woman tensed up."

Over the next two minutes, she virtually melted under his strong caresses. He asked, "Feeling more relaxed now, honey?"

"Yes, thank you. You're very skilled, Mr. Bruce."

"Practice makes perfect. I have to be alone in my private office right now. I'll be thinking about you, Molly."

He trotted to the elevator.

I walked back to Molly and asked, "Trying to make me jealous?"

"Do you want Mr. Bruce to give you a back rub?"

"You know what I mean. You're playing hard to get, then cozying up to the big boss in front of me. Nice try, Molly."

VI

Another Sunday rolled around, with few clients. Molly folded shirts, generally keeping her back to me. Chelsea joined her. I watched for customers.

The door opened and brought us a unique sight. A portly man, about 70 years old, waddled in. He had round, bulging eyes like someone with Grave's Disease. I found it especially distracting that he had a literally painted-on silver moustache and eyebrows. He also colored in his hairline with a blue eyebrow pencil.

Chelsea whispered, "Hey, Molly, it's Mister Bantam. I wonder what he brought us today."

"Maybe a half-dead kitty."

I whispered, "What's going on?"

Molly spoke to me for the first time in several days: "That's Mr. Bantam. He's generous to a fault—and it's all his fault. In mid-January, he brought us a half-eaten chocolate cake with icing that said, 'Happy New Y—'"

Miles walked in and stood next to me. Mr. Bantam hefted his way over, fixed his fish-eyes on me and said, "Hello, Miles."

Miles popped around me and said, "Hi, Mr. Bantam. Can I help you?"

Mr. Bantam handed him a chocolate doughnut.

Miles looked at the two bites in the pastry and said a flat, "Oh. Thanks."

"I don't see so well," said Mr. Bantam.

Miles discreetly dropped the contaminated doughnut into a wastebasket.

Mr. Bantam asked, "And since my vision is shot, can you take me to the little boys' room?"

Miles grimaced, but then his eyes lit up, "I'll get Byron. Just a minute."

I had a bad feeling about this. Byron's burnout had not improved lately, so it seemed like an invitation to disaster to have him deal with such an eccentric person.

Byron walked in, as stiff as the tin man, but then smiled and loosened up. "Oh, hello, Mr. Bantam."

"My good Lord Byron, can you guide me to the Gentlemen's Lounge?"

"With pleasure. Just take a hold of my arm."

"You're a good man, Byron."

Rolly rode down the escalator, and watched the image of Byron in a herring-bone gray suit, walking arm-in-arm with the weirdly made-up figure in a dirty, black raincoat and rumpled black pants with mud on the cuffs.

Rolly asked his girlfriend, "Chelsea, was that Byron's grandfather?"

"No, but he's one of the only customers Byron likes any more."

"Why is that?"

"You can purchase Byron's loyalty."

"Oh?"

"Mr. Bantam always tips Byron $10, even if he makes a return."

"Really? Does Mr. Bantam like music?"

"I immerse myself in your music. If I do, he will."

"I'll have to talk to Mr. Bantam. Maybe he'll buy one of my albums."

"He'll talk you to death before you can open your mouth."

Byron and Mr. Bantam returned a couple minutes later. The latter prosed on: "And then I learned about how they make Zegna suits. That Italian company does pick stitching on the lapels, which I can't see any more. I also love the luxurious feel of that Bemburg lining."

They kept walking to the suit department, with Bantam talking non-stop.

Rolly commented to Chelsea, "He's a weird old man."

"No, honey, we call him eccentric."

"What's the difference?"

"If you're poor, you're weird; if you're rich, you're eccentric."

"Then he can invest in my rock opera about the Creature."

Molly looked up from her straightening, smiled sweetly, and said, "Rolly, some of us remember your previous show, at least those of us who sat through it."

"*Rescuing St. Nick* was a classic, Molly."

"You premiered in an 800 seat theater, and only 100 people showed up for opening night. Then 60 people came for the pay-what-you-can night."

"And they loved it," said Rolly.

"Most of the audience left shaking their heads. The tactful ones called it 'interesting.'"

"It was the best weekend I ever had."

"Which is how long it ran. Your investors weren't happy."

"It's not like I ripped anyone off. I paid them back from the money I made fishing in Alaska."

"Oh, I know you didn't actually defraud them. You had spent most of their money on that cast album, yet virtually nothing on publicity."

"Right, I learned my lesson. And I appreciate your concern. I'll always feel sentimental about you."

Chelsea piped up, "That's how you know he's a genius; he's still learning."

"Besides," said Rolly, "I'm hooked up with a special lady who's got business brains. I want a hit play. And my next musical will go to Broadway."

"Well, in the meantime," said Molly, "shouldn't you get a higher paying job than playing the piano here?"

"Not yet. I've got a business meeting with a backer, Mr. Bantam."

"You're like a panhandler," scoffed Molly, "Do you realize that?"

"No, I'm a risk taker, like this." He leaped up on the cash register table, then did an imitation of a tightrope walk. Rolly hopped back down, gave Chelsea a peck on the cheek, and said, "I'll be right back." He left for points unknown.

Chelsea said to me, "I've got a whole collage of him doing his tightrope routine all over town, on concrete walls, banisters, balconies. Rolly is a man of action. Never say never, never say die. When he makes up his mind to do something, no one can talk him out of it; not lawyers, not doctors, not investors, not accountants, not his parents. Those meddlers strengthen his resolve."

I asked, "Can he talk you out of anything, like an education?"

"He doesn't need to. I want to spend all my free time with him."

"What about medical school?"

"Then I wouldn't have time for a relationship with the man of my dreams."

"What about all the science and Latin you studied?"

"He says I can translate one of his rock operas into Latin."

"You're building your world around him."

"Nothing can tear me away from Rolly."

"Chelsea, when I came back to work here, I said that you had more potential than any of your colleagues. I meant it. Where can you go as a department store saleswoman? The best you can hope for is Manhattan or Beverly Hills. And even then, you're still just a servant waiting on spoiled rich people. But if you're a doctor, the whole world will open up for you; high pay and opportunities in far away places."

"I don't plan to work here forever."

"Good. Where do you see yourself in five years?"

"Rolly said I'll be President and CEO of his company. He'll run the artistry, and I'll run the business end."

"Medical school is better."

"Why spend ten years in school when my real happiness is with him? He has real ambition. We'll rule Broadway together."

"That's not where I see you in five years, if you stay with him. I picture you pregnant, with a two-year-old squalling in a playpen, stuffed animals and plastic cars scattered all over the worn carpet of a cramped apartment. Meanwhile, Rolly will stay out later and later, partying with gorgeous actresses. You won't seem so fun and pretty to him any more. He'll drop you for one of those girls, but he'll be really nice about it."

Chelsea stretched to her full height of 5'2" and put her hands on her hips. "I resent that. You don't know Rolly; I do."

"I've known a lot of men like Rolly. I was one of those men. Don't make mistakes like we did. Your father would be more proud of you as a physician than as a supporting character in Rolly's life."

"My father is always proud of me. Rolly is my ambition. Rolly is my bliss."

She held her head back, a look of calm defiance on her lovely face.

I returned to folding pants at a different table. Chelsea had won that round, but I knew how to manage her life.

Mr. Bantam and Byron emerged from the corridor of the fitting rooms, about twenty minutes later. Byron actually followed the standard company suggestions: he complimented Mr. Bantam on his purchase, told him the sports jacket would be ready in two days, and thanked him for being such a loyal customer.

Mr. Bantam not only held out a credit card, but a bill: "Here's a little gratuity."

"Oh, no sir," said Byron, "that's a twenty; you never tip more than a ten."

"Always looking out for me. Take the twenty as a reward for your honesty. My best friends work in this department store. I've got lots of friends: cashiers, cab drivers, baristas, bank tellers, and Mormon missionaries."

And then Rolly intruded, "Hello, Mr. Bantam. I'm Rolly Harris, Chelsea McGuffin's boyfriend."

"Do you work here?"

"I play the piano upstairs. Can I accompany you to your next destination?"

"I'm going to get a cappuccino."

"I'll walk you over." Rolly took Mr. Bantam's right arm.

At first, Byron had appeared shocked, but his wide eyes and raised eyebrows soon turned into a frown. Not to be outdone, Byron grabbed Mr. Bantam's left bicep, and said, "I can do that."

"It's okay, Byron," said Rolly.

"No, it isn't."

A tug-of-war ensued, each one trying to pull the strangely painted figure closer to himself.

Rolly's usually sunny demeanor vanished. He said to Byron: "You should clean that fitting room."

"I already have."

"Don't you have the rest of your job to get back to?"

"I'm doing it now, Rolly. Mr. Bantam is my customer."

"He's my investor."

Mr. Bantam broke in: "I'm what?"

Before the competition could resume, Miles showed up and said, "Byron, I need to talk to you."

Byron relinquished his hold on Mr. Bantam and trudged over to Miles.

Rolly said to the customer, "Mr. Bantam, I have a golden opportunity for you to become a patron of the arts, and make a profit."

They made a great team, as they walked out the door. Mr. Bantam's globular eyes, blue-penciled hairline, and silver-painted eyebrows and moustache complemented Rolly's two-toned orange and brown wavy locks, and soul patch on his chin.

I looked back to observe two other men. Byron Davenport wore his light gray, herringbone suit and gold necktie. His color scheme and style clashed with Miles. The department manager wore jeans and a blue plaid sports jacket, with an open necked shirt.

They would soon clash in more ways than dressing style.

Miles asked, "So how much did Mr. Bantam buy today?"

Byron lit up, at first. "It was great. He purchased a Zegna blazer, which set him back four figures. It was the best sale I've made all week."

"That's it?" asked Miles, flatly, "Just one item?"

"One expensive item." Byron's rarely seen smile disappeared.

Miles lectured, "That's not how our system operates. You don't sell just one item. You show him shirts and ties. Bring up your Units Per Transaction. It's part of why you're likely to lose this job."

"He couldn't see the shirts and ties. He was more interested in how the garment felt, inside and out. The luxurious wool and the softness of the lining were what appealed to him."

"You should have done it anyway for practice. Not only that, but you have to maintain contact. Have you thought of calling customers at home?"

"I thought of it. I considered it. I rejected it."

"Why's that?"

"It seems intrusive. Customers need us to respect their privacy."

"That attitude will cost you your job here."

Miles walked away, and Byron fumed.

The next time I glanced in Byron's direction, he was folding polo shirts.

Chelsea walked over and held out a Navy blue suit with chalk marks all over the back of it, and on the sleeves. A long alterations ticket dangled from the hanger's hook. "Byron? Did you have this on hold for a customer last week?"

Byron's face hardened, and his eyes blazed into total focus. He snatched the ticket and attempted to rip it off. Instead, the ticket stayed on the hanger and he pulled Chelsea against his body.

Byron leaped backwards and his anger turned into apparent embarrassment. He said hastily: "I'm sorry, Chelsea. I was trying to yank the ticket off."

"It's okay."

Miles sauntered up five feet behind Byron, and watched.

I sorted through topcoats, sizing them correctly on the rack. It gave me a good view of the proceedings.

Byron complained to Chelsea, "I spent a half hour with that customer. A tailor marked the jacket. I took the piker all the way to the cash register, started ringing him up, and then came buyer's remorse. The piker says, 'I want to think about it.' That's the kiss of death."

Miles asked from behind Byron, "How will you change your sales technique?"

Byron did a silent movie reaction. He leaped up and his eyes bugged out. He whirled around and asked Miles, "Who are you, Inspector Javert?"

"Who?"

"From *Les Miserables* by Victor Hugo."

"From what?"

"Never mind."

Miles said, "Chelsea, will you give us a minute?"

She set off on another chore, and I flashed her a grin of encouragement.

Once again, Miles lectured Byron: "You need to ask yourself what you could have done differently with the client. He works for you. Once he comes in here, he's not supposed to have any free will. How did you blow the sale at the last minute?"

"Maybe I was too nice to the piker."

"I find that hard to believe. Now, I'll ask you again since you still haven't answered: how will you change your sales technique?"

Byron sighed, looked down, looked back up, and knotted his eyebrows. He replied, "I'll just have to kill one of the customers."

"What?!"

"It'll send a message to the other pikers."

"You can't mean that."

"This is a real innovation, Miles: selling through terror."

"You're sick!"

"Yes, I'm sick."

Molly came down the escalator, and walked right between the young men toward the cash register, as if not noticing the debate.

Byron continued, "I didn't mean a word of what I just said. But my scenario is every bit as realistic as the company's training."

"Human resources will hear about this."

Our manager headed toward the elevator.

Meanwhile, Byron held forth, looking in Miles Roomer's direction, then into my eyes, and toward Molly. She never looked up from organization of receipts.

"That's fine by me, Miles. Tell the shoo-flies in HR. They'll just fill out a form and file it away. You hang the Sword of Damocles over my head about customers who don't come in. I'm willing to wait for them. You're the one showing desperation, not me. Customers don't read a manual. They don't watch training videos, either. Something's got to be done about rote-memory managers, and piano players who horn in on my territory."

Fortunately, no customers heard him. He clocked out for a meal break and marched to the elevators.

I sidled over to Molly and whispered, "That was some diatribe."

"What do you mean?"

"Byron. Didn't you hear his tirade?"

"Byron does that every other week. Ignore him, and maybe he'll stop. It hurts morale."

"I don't care about the message, but it says a lot about the messenger. After all, a twisted mind is a terrible thing to waste."

VII

I came back after lunch and saw our whole team on the sales floor. Molly stood with Chelsea, pointing out some new silk shirts on hangers. Miles bent over a tall table, while writing a report.

Molly marched over to me and said, "One of the morning shift women is furious with you. Her face is as red as a fire engine; she's hyperventilating, but won't talk about what you said. She keeps spewing four-letter words about what she wishes would happen to you."

"Whom exactly do you mean?"

"The small brunette, the same age as Chelsea."

I smirked. "Mission accomplished."

"What did you do, sadist?"

"That girl had been spreading vicious lies. Gossip threatens the morale of fellow employees. I merely reacted to her behavior. First, she accused Byron of laziness. You know that's a distortion. He's always cleaning and straightening, if he isn't failing to sell something to a customer. Then that female rotter said I must be on prescription meds. That's not only slanderous, it's actionable. But the worst was what she said about Chelsea."

Molly leaned forward, put her hands on her hips and said slowly, "What about Chelsea?"

"The gossip-monger said that Chelsea used her pretty face and 'slinky little body' to rack up bigger sales."

Molly tightened her jaw and sucked in her lips. I could tell that my alleged victim had lost Molly's sympathy.

I continued, "That final bit of slander burned me more than anything else. No one badmouths Chelsea McGuffin on my watch."

Molly nodded in approval. "Did you tell Miles?"

"Tell Miles and you've told the wall. When I brought up the problem, he said, 'You're both adults. You handle it.' That's another cliché from the manual."

"You sound like Byron."

"Byron can't be wrong about everything. And Miles only got worse."

"How?"

"Miles defended the gossip monger, saying it was her way of making sure other people were doing their fair share. Can you believe that? First he tells me to handle it, then gives the lying little brat authority over me."

"What did you do, Jim?"

"I used psychology." I looked around to make sure Miles didn't sneak up on me, then gave my explanation to Molly. "I said to the gossip monger, 'My dear, your hostility reeks of envy.'

"She scoffed at first, Then I said, 'The other women here, like Molly and Chelsea, are beautiful works of art. You are nothing but a dumpy little drudge, with no real future. Your only dates will be with drunks who'll heave you out of bed when the liquor wears off.'

"Now, Molly, if that toad-faced little gossip takes offense at honest evaluation by a professional, then it's her own fault."

I couldn't tell by the stony expression on Molly's face if she was fascinated or sickened. She said, "Do me a favor, Jim." I waited for the cutting witticism: "Don't volunteer on a suicide hotline."

"Give me two more conversations with that gossip monger, and I'll make her resign."

"That won't be necessary."

Molly broke away from me, and returned to Chelsea and the silk shirts.

Not long thereafter, Byron walked up to Miles and said, "That idiot from the stock room just dumped four huge boxes on our floor. He said, 'Here, buddy, take care of them.' They're not even for this department."

"How do you know?

"I opened them. They're for the 'Home Sweet Home' section upstairs. He was just too damn lazy to take them up there himself."

"What's inside?"

The elevator bell rang, and Rolly bounded out. He made a big announcement, so I didn't hear what was in the large boxes.

"I did it!" exclaimed Rolly, "After a two hour presentation, Mr. Bantam is going to back my show."

Molly asked, "Do you mean you talked to him that long?"

"No," Rolly explained, "I talked for five minutes, sang for five minutes, and then Mr. Bantam talked for an hour and fifty minutes. I couldn't follow most of it. We got back on topic long enough for him to write a check to my business. My director and I will meet him again tomorrow."

Byron tilted his head sideways, and asked, "How much money are we talking?"

"Enough to rent an 800-seat theater, with a huge fish tank at downstage center. That's where the leading lady will swim. We'll have a false bottom, so the Creature can look up at her, but the actor isn't really submerged. I'll also need an orchestra on risers, with two pianos, a cellist, a guitarist, and a banjo player."

Molly inquired, "How's the Creature from the Black Lagoon supposed to sing?"

"Sing?" Rolly echoed, "Sing? Don't be far-fetched. The Creature will play the big drum kit at upstage center. He can really rock out. Every song will be an essay about either love or ecology. Mr. Bantam is going to pay for recording the cast album, too."

Byron muttered, "Why is this happening?"

Molly patted his shoulder and said, "Face it, Byron. Rolly has a gift for convincing rich people to invest in his projects. He believes so strongly in what he's doing that it gives him contagious confidence."

"Strange, isn't it?" asked Byron, "If I apply at a business and ask to work hard in order to earn money, I'm a loser. If Rolly begs for money for some unproduced project, he's a genius."

Rolly reminded us: "I've had ten shows produced professionally."

"Paying actors in gift cards doesn't count," Molly retorted.

"It did to Chelsea. She made a lot of commission."

Byron said, "Why couldn't you find someone else to back your latest masterpiece?"

"They already know him," replied Molly.

Byron led Miles to the incorrectly delivered boxes, but the rest of us stayed in Rolly's orbit of euphoria.

Euphoric people can do foolish things.

Rolly continued, "Mr. Bantam is excited about this play. Who would have imagined that *The Creature from the Black Lagoon* was his favorite movie?"

"There is a resemblance," said Molly.

"Mr. Bantam stopped people in the coffee line to tell them about his project. That was when I said goodbye. I was so thrilled afterward, I did my trademark high wire act on concrete partitions and hand rails. I have great balance."

Chelsea basked in his glow: "You're an inspiration."

"So was the Creature. He inspires me to write great music. Now I'm going to do the tight rope routine on the cash wrap desk. Whoo!"

I hadn't heard him shout, "Whoo" before. But his tightrope stunt looked like a golden opportunity. I said, "Rolly, you shouldn't do that."

He said, "Why not? I'm so happy, I'm going to do this act on the highest level."

Rolly looked up toward the 4th floor.

I countered, "No you're not, it's too dangerous."

Chelsea said, "I love you, Rolly. This is how you swept me off my feet. I love the excitement."

"Rolly, I forbid you to go up there."

He hopped down from the desk, put his face one inch from mine and announced, "I'm a risk taker. I follow my bliss. Whoo!"

Then he dashed for the escalator. A $50,000 check in his pocket must have triggered a full-blown manic episode.

Chelsea ran after her boyfriend.

Byron left the boxes. I said to him, "That interjection *whoo* is annoying. Am I right?"

"Yes, Mr. Western."

"I hate to correct you, Byron, but that's Doctor Western."

Byron nodded, and didn't react otherwise. I tried an experiment by shouting, "Whoo! It does create an endorphin reaction, like a runner's high. Maybe that's why Rolly does it. This could lead to addictive or compulsive symptoms."

"Maybe you can use him in a seminar," said Byron, "I've got to stalk the pikers."

He walked away, leaving me confused. I said to Molly, "What?"

"Byron means 'serve the customers.'"

"Chelsea translates what Byron says in Latin, and you translate what he says in English. What exactly is a piker?"

"A petty cheapskate."

"That rules me out." The phone rang, and I answered it. Byron's voice came on the line, so I hung up the phone. I looked around and saw no sign of anyone on our floor. "Well, Molly, we're alone at last. Why don't we slip into the fitting room together, for old time's sake?"

"Forget it, Jim."

"I can't. And neither can you."

A loud, extended shout of "whoo" came from above us.

I looked up and performed play-by-play commentary for Molly's benefit: "Rolly and Chelsea are headed up in the escalator. She's standing on a higher step, so he doesn't have to bend too far to kiss her. I surmise that the cries of delight affect his head in a positive manner, while the kisses bathe his heart in endorphins. That's how you used to make me feel." Molly straightened out neck ties on a drum table, but didn't respond. I continued, "Chances are he gets a rush of adrenaline from his amateur tightrope act he's about to do up there on the 4th floor. I'll bet you're wondering how I know this." I waited for a response, which didn't come: "I once wrote a seminar paper on body chemistry and presented it at a conference in Chicago."

"That's interesting," Molly replied in a leaden tone.

"Oh, I get it. You're tuning out my mini-lecture like you do with Byron's verbal tantrums."

Her silence confirmed my assessment. I looked up again and commented, "That's odd. There goes Chelsea's other swain, Byron, charging up the escalator. Make a note of that."

"Why bother?"

"Maybe he'll challenge Rolly to a duel."

"Did you put that in Byron's mind?"

"I can't control someone like Byron. But I can predict Rolly. So can you."

"Just leave me out of it. I was a fool to interfere in that relationship. Chelsea is completely besotted; and Rolly does the exact opposite of what anyone suggests."

"I noticed. Chelsea needs to become a physician, to make her father proud."

"She's probably more careful than," Molly stopped, glanced around, and said softly, "You know who."

"Not necessarily. Rolly the Svengali will get her preggers before she earns a degree."

"Are you sure of that?"

"Dead certain," I said with a smile, "unless someone intercedes. Excuse me."

I broke away from my conversation with Molly. We no longer stood together on the ground floor.

Meanwhile, Rolly had indeed mounted the slender rail, and did a veritable tight rope routine, with his arms stretched out horizontally, like a condor's wings. On his right was the safety of the 4th floor, on his left was a 40 foot drop. He shouted: "Whoo! Take my picture!" shouted Rolly, "Take my picture."

He sounded like kids in a developing country when they meet tourists. Chelsea called out, "I'd have to get my camera, baby."

"I love you!" shouted Rolly.

"I love you more!"

"Blow me a kiss."

"I'll blow you a hug!"

How nauseating.

And where was everybody? No customers, no salespeople, no immigration agents to roust the tailors. I wondered how I could make someone come to our floor.

"Follow your bliss. Whoo!" shouted Rolly.

And then he fell.

VIII

After the paramedics took Rolly away on a gurney, Molly and I launched a discussion of the case. I said, "Do you see who was there to hug Chelsea first, after Rolly's folly?"

"You?"

"No. Byron Davenport. Significant, isn't it? We don't know what all went down." I couldn't help smiling.

"You've been acting smug, and dropping hints."

"Dropping hints? That's a poor choice of words. Don't make me your fall guy, pun intended."

"You've been back at the store for a few weeks, and someone met with a terrible accident."

"He was nothing but a hanger-on."

"No, Jim, I consider you the hanger-on in my life. That's how I know your mindset so well."

"Just how well do you know it?"

"If you thought you could get away with it, you'd commit a recreational murder."

I didn't know quite how to take that. I would have said to it was a compliment, but Molly probably meant it as censure. I said, "Don't get above yourself, salesgirl."

"My theory gratifies your massive ego. Here's how I see it: Rolly was doing his tightrope act on the handrail. You took the elevator to the third floor, just beneath where he stood. Then you whipped out your tape measure, lassoed it around his ankle, gave a tug, and down he fell."

"Nice try, Miss Marple, but I didn't do anything like that."

Miles walked out of the back room and joined our conference. "Did either of you see what happened?"

I said, "We both heard it. Molly here doesn't think it was accidental. If this was a homicide then it had to be someone with a motive. Someone jealous and unstable."

I timed my theory impeccably. Byron walked over to us and said to Miles, "A seemingly happy man does himself a violence. You all thought it would be me, just because of my threats. That's not it at all. I don't want to commit suicide, but it's required by forces beyond my control."

"Will you be quiet?" said Miles, "This isn't about you."

"No, it's about Rolly," Byron answered, "I read his thoughts. He was going to trick my customer into losing his money on a rock opera. He planned to have Mister Bantam pay for his wedding to Chelsea. That was how Rolly expected to climax opening night, with the Creature performing the ceremony."

"Did Rolly say that?"

"No, but he thought it."

"I want you off this sales floor. You probably pushed Rolly."

"Not directly. I subconsciously willed it to happen with telekinesis. My thoughts traveled to him and he fell like Icarus, who flew too close to the sun."

"You sick bastard! That's virtually a confession. You pushed Rolly so you could take up with Chelsea."

"You're out of your mind, Miles."

"Look who's talking. You were jealous of Rolly. You have a crush on Chelsea."

"That's not true."

"You were always hanging around her. We all saw it. Byron, you never could compete with an accomplished, talented man like Rolly. I saw you heading upstairs after them."

I chimed in, "So did I."

"And so did Jim," said Miles, "Byron, you must have sneaked up behind Rolly and Chelsea. You probably threw a pen at the back of his head, he moved to the left, and lost his balance. Then while Chelsea looked down in horror, you rushed up and hugged her. You were suddenly the big, strong man in her hour of grief. What do you say to that?"

"You're more creative than I thought."

"Your statement about killing customers was more than gallows humor. It showed your true nature. You, Byron Davenport, you did it." He clapped his hand on Byron's shoulder.

Byron shook Miles Roomer's hand off and growled, "Don't lie about me."

"You never could take criticism either."

"Sure I can. You can trash me all you like with the truth. Trash me with lies and I'll go ballistic."

"Admit it, you pushed Rolly!"

"Subconscious telekinesis."

"And you did it out of jealousy."

"I envied the way he could get rich people to part with their money. I'll grant you that."

"And you're in love with Chelsea."

"I'm not in love with Chelsea, I'm in love with Molly."

Molly's eyes widened to the size of quarters. "What!?"

"Damn it!" snapped Byron. "Miles used an old interrogator's trick. He tells a lie, then I correct him with the truth. I only hung around with Chelsea so Molly wouldn't know about my feelings for her. Molly would have rejected me and I'd have been humiliated."

"Like now?" asked Molly. She directed sarcasm at our manager, "Nice going, Miles."

Miles looked from Byron to Molly and said, "Wait a minute. I'm confused. I couldn't follow any of what Byron just said."

I interpreted for him: "Somewhere in that hodgepodge, Byron admitted to pining for Molly Daniels."

"Byron isn't the only one who's embarrassed," Molly commented. The phone rang, and she answered it.

Miles took on an uncommonly commanding presence, with ramrod straight posture, and a forceful tone. "Well, Byron, you've got more to worry about than embarrassment. You're going to prison."

He wrapped his arms around Byron's shoulders from behind.

Byron shouted, "Take your hands off me!"

"It's all up to me. I feel like Sherlock Holmes."

"More like Inspector Lestrade."

"Who?"

Molly hung up the phone and shouted, "Stop it, Miles, you're upsetting him."

Miles responded, "He admitted pushing Rolly, even if it was through ESP."

But Molly wasn't to be dissuaded: "Byron was nowhere near Rolly when it happened."

Miles released Byron and walked to Molly, "What about his partial confession?"

"He'd blame himself for the Kennedy assassination right now."

Byron gazed in the full-length mirror: "When I look in the glass, I see the devil looking back at me."

Miles said to Molly, "How do you know where he was?"

"That was Customer Service on the phone just now. They wanted to tell us about a different problem. When Rolly was tightrope-walking upstairs, Byron was at the customer service window, giving his side of a complaint against him. Some gentleman objected to being called a piker. In fact, the client mistook it for another word altogether."

You'd think that Molly's hearsay evidence would calm the situation, but the mayhem increased with my participation. Molly insisted it meant that Byron had an airtight alibi. But even Byron wouldn't let it go. He said to us, "I guess that rules me out physically."

Miles turned to me and said, "You're a psychologist, Jim. What's your professional diagnosis of Byron?"

"He's crazy."

Miles nodded and grinned, as if finding validation from an expert witness, then marched back to Byron, "Jim is right about you."

"I'm not crazy," said Byron, "I'm stressed out from people plotting against me. Keep your hands off me, Miles."

Byron reached under his sports jacket, and whipped out a dark object. He sprayed Miles in the face with some foul-smelling liquid.

Miles shouted, "My eyes!"

The manager's orbs and nose ran disgustingly. I took charge. "Miles, you'd better head to the back room to the sink, and wash out your tear ducts. Molly, take this atypical psychotic to a quiet place."

Miles scurried away, covering his face, and coughing like a TB patient.

I wondered how Molly would deal with a madman who could easily become a lifelong stalker if she let him down easily, or a revenge-driven maniac if her rejection was too harsh. She said, "Byron, we have to break up and remain on friendly terms. You can refer to me as your ex-girlfriend from now on."

"How can you say that? Women find me repellent."

"That's not true Byron. Remember all those lunches we had in the cafeteria? You can count them as dates. You're a much nicer man than my other ex-boyfriend who works here."

She flashed daggers at me with her eyes.

Molly wasn't done yet, "Byron, I have another man I'm interested in. You have the courage to take my rejection in a dignified and chivalrous way. I once read a poem by Richard Lovelace called, 'To Lucasta, Going to the Wars.' He ends with:

> "I could not love thee, Dear, so much
> Loved I not honor more."

After a long silence, Byron said, "So should I. Goodbye, Molly."
He headed for the escalator, and out of our lives.

IX

The next morning brought our big meeting with Mr. Bruce. Molly already stood by him. I said, "You wanted to see me, Pinky?"

"I want more information about yesterday's accident," said Mr. Bruce.

"Poor Rolly," I said, "He had a great career of flops ahead of him. I'm surprised by your sudden interest. You delegate everything else."

"It could cost me in excess of a million dollars. Did you influence Rolly Harris to play acrobat up there?"

"I did the exact opposite. In fact, I warned him it was dangerous."

Molly confirmed it: "That's true."

I thanked her.

But then she said, "It was the perfect crime: reverse psychology as a lethal weapon."

I protested, "I didn't expect him to take a header."

"You had also tried to cajole him into making a pass at me, and you used psychological warfare on that gossip monger."

I waved Molly off, with the back of my hand pointing down in her direction: "Irrelevant. Here's what must have happened: Our friendly young maniac had the motive. Byron envied Rolly's success. Remember how he rushed up the escalator? Byron saw his opportunity to trick witnesses into providing him with an alibi. He was explaining his case about the irate client, to the Customer Service dames. Then he turned away when Rolly shouted,

'Whoo!' Byron dashed off, so the dames would think Rolly had fallen.

"But Rolly was still on the hand rail. That was when Byron embraced Chelsea. He pulled her so she had her back to Rolly. That's when Byron pushed him over the side."

Mr. Bruce said, "That doesn't make any sense."

I defended my position: "All right, then he had an accomplice. Envy, pure and simple. Combine it with his delusions and auditory hallucinations of thought projections from Rolly. What was there to stop him? Byron also had that weird fixation on Chelsea."

Molly said, "You're the one with the Chelsea fixation."

I dreaded this new direction to the conversation. I said, "Molly must be kidding."

"Don't play dumb with me," said Mr. Bruce, "I knew your family before you were born. Chelsea looks like your father's mother."

And then the jig was up. Molly said to me, for our leader's benefit: "We didn't raise our daughter, but you still want a claim on her, Jim. You didn't want a mere salesgirl for your offspring. Oh, no, she had to be the elite; someone you could brag about; an extension of yourself. Her love for Rolly stood in the way."

It's humiliating to be outwitted by someone of less education. I stood firm: "You can't touch me. I'm going to comfort that dear girl, and inspire her to become a great plastic surgeon."

My situation deteriorated even further. I would have expected Miles to sneak up on me, but instead Chelsea appeared. She shouted, "You monster!"

"I know you're sad now," I said tenderly to my biological daughter, "but look at the big picture. Rolly wasn't right for you. I want to be a positive influence on your decisions."

"Some father. You tried to kill the man of my dreams."

Something in that sentence bothered me: "Tried to?"

And that's when Rolly Harris walked in. Icarus was now Lazarus. He said, banally, "Hi, everybody."

"How?" I shouted, "I saw you fall."

"I fell into a big open box, full of comforters and pillows. The stock room guy had put them down here, instead of the Home Sweet Home Department.

That was a lucky break."

I said, "But you weren't moving."

It was as if I wanted to convince him to die after all.

Rolly explained, "Concussion. I'm okay now though. It was a real inspiration. I'm going to add a singing high diver to my next show."

I put my hands over my face. Molly said, "You seem disappointed, Jim."

Rolly told her, "I'm not mad at Jim. He told me not to do my tightrope act up there on the 4th floor."

"But he did try to pin the blame on Byron."

"Yeah, that was going a little too far. But look, Molly, Jim was nice to me. When I was balancing up there, he waved at me and I waved back. That's the last thing I remember, until I woke up in the hospital."

Molly said, "You never mentioned that, Jim."

"It didn't seem important."

Silence followed. A clock ticked in the background. I wished for anything to end this tension at my exposure. And then I was sorry for what I wished for.

Chelsea said, "You'll never guess what happened, Rolly. I've been accepted to the UW School of Business."

I shouted, "Oh, please, God, no!"

"Awesome," said Rolly, "We'll rule Broadway in five years."

They left, hand-in-hand together.

All my efforts had failed. Rolly survived and kept Chelsea's love. She would not become a physician. I looked to the one person I knew had once loved me. "Molly, why is this happening to me? All I wanted was to be a part of Chelsea's life. What should I do?"

"You could gain her attention by doing a tightrope act on the 4th floor. I'll take your picture."

That didn't lighten my mood. I asked, "What next? Will Byron announce that his lunacy was all a charade?"

"No, Byron was already deteriorating."

Mr. Bruce finally spoke again, "Well, Jim, you're right that we have one more surprise. Chelsea has an irresponsible biological father, a responsible adoptive father, but now she needs a generous step-father. Molly, will you marry me?"

"I don't know if I can give up my career," Molly replied, "Selling men's sportswear is a passion of mine. I'll have to think about it."

I struggled to regain control: "Ha! Sorry, Pinky, but you can take that as a no."

"Wrong," said Molly, "it means yes."

Multi-colored specks filled my graying vision. Molly and Mr. Bruce's faces appeared to become gigantic as they smiled upon each other. The grayness turned to blackness, and I fell to the floor.

Mr. Bruce's voice echoed through the darkness: "Did he faint, or drop dead? Shouldn't we check?"

"No, dear, you can delegate that to your lowliest serf."

"You're right, my love. Miles?"

Footsteps vibrated the carpet under my forehead, then stopped abruptly. Miles said, "Yes, Mr. Bruce?"

"Clean this up."

Monty Moudlyn

INTRODUCTION

Monty Moudlyn was a successful stage director, whose children's theater plays shattered box office records across Kitsap County, Washington. Several of his protégés went on to appear in TV series on the WB network, independent movies, short films, & commercials.

No one ever heard from Monty again, after his departure to form a peace organization called, "The Hug Brigade." Some say Monty was last seen hugging Hell's Angels at a Montana truck stop. Others claim he disappeared in Somalia, distributing embraces to warlords. And there are those who maintain that he dwells somewhere in Angola, Afghanistan, or the Congo.

This booklet contains four pivotal moments in Monty's life, before he started on his quest. A group of actors dramatized the stories for radio in a play which aired on WFHB *Firehouse Theater* in Bloomington, Indiana and KUNM *Albuquerque Radio Theater* in New Mexico.

Kyle James won the Rising Star Award at the Melbourne Independent Filmmakers Festival in Florida in 2011 for his portrayal of our hero in the short film, *The Adventures of Monty Moudlyn*. The film directed by Zach Hibbard and produced by Erik Emerick came in 2nd place for the MIFF audience award, and 3rd prize in the Enzian Theater Film Slam in that same State.

The first major event catalogued in this booklet was the untimely demise of Monty's mentor, Norman. You learn a lot about people by what they say about others. The eulogy Monty delivered was printed in issue number 18 of *A Very Small Magazine*, in 1992.

PASSAGE OF A MOUDLYN

Today I honor my comrade, counselor, and cousin, Norman Henry Moudlyn. Even as tiny tots, we were the best of buddies. I looked up to him because he was two years older, but soon my admiration grew.

Norman once saved my life. I had accidentally hurled our great-grandmother's wedding ring into a busy intersection, so I scampered after it. Before I could meet a speeding Volkswagen's fender, Norman charged over, scooped my body into his arms, and deposited me on the other side. My savior rose to his full height, shook his finger in my four year old face, and scolded, "You wisten, Monty. You just a widdle bwat, and I'se all gwo'd up. Don't pway in da stweet."

After I explained the situation, Norman retreated back into the intersection, probably hoping to rescue great granny's ring.

We had only God to thank for allowing Norman to survive the accident. The paramedics and emergency room staff also deserve some credit.

Norman provided us all with great inspiration. Thanks to him, City Hall erected a traffic light in that location; he became poster child for local driving safety classes; and a poet gave up LSD. Norman never called himself a hero. Now that I think about it, the modest martyr would have called himself an "altwooist."

My cousin changed subtly after that. Norman giggled whenever someone mentioned the word, rifle. The boy came up with a new innovation for elimination of earwigs from the mailbox: an M-80 firecracker.

And he was a gentleman. My mother told us she planned to hold a cocktail party, so Norman volunteered to purchase kerosene, bottles, and rags. All through high school, teachers apparently appreciated his good looks. They never took their eyes off him, nor did they ever turn their backs.

I know full well that, had Norman lived beyond his twenty-sixth year, he would have been revered as a deep, philosophical thinker. My kinsman told me his theory about human existence, while we sat in the shade of a venerable oak tree:

"Listen, Monty. Some people are young, but they grow out of it. Don't forget that in the big garden of life, some of us are peas, carrots, pumpkins, or whatever. And if God sees a sickly plant, or a strong, ugly weed, He lobs a grenade. When that car hit me, God probably thought I was a weed, so He pulled the pin. But you know what? That shrapnel was fertilizer, and it made me a man."

At that moment, Norman's philosophy struck me in almost the same manner as that Ford station wagon struck him. Not only had my mentor saved my life, but he also gave me a complex way of looking at it. I resolved to apply his concise wisdom to my own artistry and personal relationships.

That brings us to the present. It was a sad Fourth of July. Norman had hoped to surprise us with a homemade fertilizer bomb, which he kept under a rock in the back yard. How fortunate he didn't hide it under his bed. That way, our house remained undamaged, except the windows.

So long, old buddy.

Editor's Note

Monty persevered. After a year at Olympic Community College, he transferred to Cornish, earned his BFA in Theater Arts, and racked up numerous successes as an actor, stage director, and poet. Here we have an account of a poetry reading at the Bainbridge Island Playhouse:

MONTY MOUDLYN - POET

I savored a cavalcade of poetic offerings that eventide. For example, a teenage girl read her newest masterpiece, "Alone." We also applauded Alice Fisher's prize winner, "Death of a Hired Woman." Then came my turn. I strode to the podium, and began:

A Speculation on Fatherhood
(Someday)

My son.
He'll wear green overalls
With pictures of bunnies thereon.
My son will run outside

To play with his buddy, Dillon.
Together, they shall collaborate on
The most beautiful mud pies
I shall ever gaze upon.

For a son of mine will be marvelous.
A son of mine will be dear.
The jam stains on his cheeks and lips
Will be cute when he is near.

"Thank you," I concluded, "I am Monty Moudlyn."

After the recital, I received the most powerful reaction from any audience, anywhere. Silence. One hundred literary patrons stared at me in reverent contemplation. Some glanced at each other. One lady's mouth gaped in wonder.

How long could I bask in the moment? Should I follow up with another poem? No. That wouldn't be fair to my fellow colleagues in verse. I smiled to the crowd again. Other poets needed their moment in the sun, too.

That decision was a learning experience. No matter how great my achievement, I must always remember to share the stage.

Editor's Note

Life wasn't always easy. Our friend also experienced romantic heartbreak. He first penned the following reminiscence in 1984, and saw its publication nine years later in *The Ecphorizer, a Mensa Magazine of Literature & Ideas*. It was one of two stories adapted in the eighteen minute film, *The Adventures of Monty Moudlyn*, with Kyle James as the title character.

OUR LAST RENDEZVOUS

I choose to speak of Elsa Chilton, my lost love. So many times, I had wanted to take her in my arms and whisper those proverbial sweet nothings. We met in our old rendezvous spot, a sun-soaked field of daisies.

She asked, "How are you, Monty?"

"Oh, my red haired beauty, just look around you. It's the most beautiful day since the dawn of time. Not a cloud in the sky. Oh, the joy of living! By the way, how are you?"

I didn't even hear the reply. I gazed deeply into Elsa's clear, green eyes, and said, "How wonderful."

"What do you mean 'how wonderful'? I just told you how upset I am."

Directing countless children's theater plays had taught me the magic of ad libbing:

"What I mean is, how wonderful you are. Besides, this triangular affair makes our love all the more romantic. You may feel sad now, but it's always darkest before the dawn. Some day, we'll look back on this traumatic time and laugh until our heads fall off."

I placed my hands on Elsa's delicate shoulders, and drew her closer. My voice spoke ever so truthfully: "I love you, honey, and I always have."

"But darling," she protested in a soft voice, "I am still betrothed to Jubal Lee."

"I don't give a darn. That bisexual professor of scatology isn't for you."

I held her close, and our lips pressed lightly together. Sunlight, the meadow, and Elsa's smile enveloped my soul. These are the elements of paradise. I asked, "Do you love me?"

"Oh, you big schnook," she said tenderly, "Of course I do."

"It's a match made in Heaven. I wish I could hold you like this forever."

The daisies seemed to play a song ascribed to King Henry VIII. A reflex action from direction of musicals made me join in the chorus:

> Greensleeves was all my joy,
> Greensleeves was my delight.
> Greensleeves was my heart of gold,
> And who but My Lady—AAACK!

My rapture was ruptured by a blow to the face, which sent me reeling. Daisies swirled in every direction, as if the planet had stepped on an emergency brake. Grass rushed up to greet me. I rolled over, looked up, and saw Elsa loom over my prostrate body.

"Forget it, Monty. I did love you until I remembered that everything about you is a cliché. You speak in clichés; you sing in clichés. Besides that, you're lousy in bed."

"Did I not smile enough?"

She left that question unanswered.

I asked, "Are you going back to Jubal?"

"No, I can do so much better than either one of you."

She kicked me in the ribs. I writhed.

"Elsa, honey, you're making a big mistake."

Another kick.

"Oh, well, Elsa. It's better to have loved and lost than to have never loved at all."

Editor's Note

Monty wasn't unattached for long. Single mothers of aspiring stars love a handsome man of action. Monty agreed with one girlfriend that her son, Chris, should audition for a musical based on an uplifting literary masterpiece. This led indirectly to yet another important turning point.

Monty wrote this account in 1989, and saw it published in *The Echporizer* in 1991. It was also part of Zach Hibbard's aforementioned cinematic accomplishment, featuring Bjorn Jiskoot as the second male lead in:

THE GLADDENING OF MICHA'S HEART

Whenever I see young people in love, it gladdens my heart. Seeing folks who enjoy their work provides even more satisfaction. I direct all children's plays for the Performers' Light Opera. That is only a secondary feature in my life. I regard myself as a lay-psychologist.

One of my dearest best friends is Micha Hamilphane, Jr., who directs mature plays in our County. On a sweltering summer day, we reached a critical moment in our friendship. We had already worked together for eleven years, ever since those carefree, happy days in community college.

I encountered Micha, standing in front of the theater. He wore a frown, so I sprang into action.

"Why, hello, Micha, how's it going?"

"The usual," he sighed, "How's your show, Monty?"

"It's glorious. Who would have ever thought that a cast of fourth graders could perform *Twelve Angry Men*? It's such a very unique challenge."

"Yes, especially since half the kids in it are girls."

While bestowing that compliment, Micha's facial expression did not change. With a note of true sincerity, I asked, "Don't you feel sunshiny?"

"Look, Monty, I don't feel much like talking."

"Are you in a sour mood?"

"Sort of. I'd rather be alone right now."

"We've been friends a long time."

"I know, but listen."

"I'm on your side all the way."

"Fine, but I just don't—"

"Is something bothering you?"

He glared up into my face, "Other than your presence?"

I secretly rejoiced. Thanks to me, he could make eye contact again. I placed my hand on his round shoulder and asked, "How long has it been since our last heart-to-heart chat?"

"Not long enough."

Just about anyone else would have walked away, at that point. However, I could peer deeper into Micha's troubled soul. Surliness, from any human being, is a cry for help; therefore I chose to remain. I said, "Open up, old fellow. Let it out. I know it hurts."

The two of us sat down on a bench. Not far away, a banner hung from the eaves. It announced, "COME & SEE *CRIME & PUNISHMENT: THE MUSICAL.* FUN FOR THE WHOLE FAMILY." Micha lingered after a day of rehearsal.

My compatriot's eyebrows looked like the separated lines of an X.

Frowns trigger the opposite effect on me. I said, "If current events disturb you, you're not alone. Maybe it's your outlook on life. Don't brood about how bad the world is; think of how splendid it can be. Imagine everyone loving each other. What would our planet be like if we all wore a happy face?"

"Boring."

I resolved then and there to ease Micha's melancholia. How terrible he looked, all hunched over. His stomach pushed out against his red T-shirt. I expected to see the garment burst. I asked, "Is your play in tip-top condition?"

"It's okay."

He glared at my sandals. I'm rather proud of my long, narrow feet. His hard eyes were like a magnifying glass, condensing a sunray into destructive weaponry. I interjected, "Phew! It sure is hot out here."

"Nothing gets by you."

I was thrilled beyond my wildest dreams. We had finally found a topic to agree on.

"All right, I guess you won't leave until I talk, so here goes. I'm burnt out on plays, life, and community theater. Actors, make up, masking flats, choreography, stress; it's making me crazy. There are a lot of other things lately, too. One of those stage mothers demanded I put little Chris in the show. You know, in the horse number? It wouldn't be so bad, but she comes to every rehearsal, calls me at home, and she's—"

"Micha, my girlfriend—I mean—the woman loves her child, and it should warm your heart the way it warms mine. Think of it as an inspiration. Character assassination won't help in the long run."

"Will you just hear me out?"

While Micha spoke, I thought up the perfect remedy. Upon his conclusion, my speech began: "I've directed plays every bit as long as you, and I never feel burnt out. Do you know why? Because, unlike so many folks, I appreciate the little things in life. A theater company is just as united as any family unit. Make up girls, grips, directors, actors, and yes, even choreographers, are the sisters and brothers, moms and dads, aunts and uncles, nuts and bolts of a family. Oh, Micha, it gives me such a lump in my throat whenever I am forced to say, 'Guys, it's been a beautiful show. Strike the set.' We labored in a battle of love when building it, and we've got the same love when we destroy it."

Micha hoisted himself up and said, "Thanks, Monty, but I've got to go right now."

"Please stay. There's more."

Micha waddled toward his Chevy pick up, with me following close behind. I was tempted to snatch his ponytail, like pulling a horse's reins, but it proved unnecessary. It's obvious that, subconsciously, Micha wanted to listen. Otherwise, he would not have let me catch up so easily.

"Good grief," he wheezed, "I've got to lose weight. I'm really out of shape."

Soon enough, we reached the vehicle. When I advised him to lick the jolly side of this lollypop called life, Micha said, "Look, Monty, I've got an appointment. There's no time, and I just don't want to talk any more. Savvy?"

"But I know better."

My colleague thrust a hand into his Levi's right front pocket, and produced a key ring. He selected one, wedged it into the lock, and opened the door. However, instead of getting inside immediately, he stood there and panted. I recognized this as a signal, so I bent down and stepped ahead. A familiar arm shot out, barring my path. Micha inquired, "What the heck are you doing?"

"Strengthening our friendship."

"Out of the way!" He glared again, shoved me aside, and plopped onto the vinyl seat. When Micha removed his hand from my flank, I became conscious of a film of perspiration between flannel and flesh. I soon felt that same layer all over my body.

Micha slammed the door, switched on the ignition, and backed up. I walked alongside.

"Please, let me tell you a simple anecdote," I shouted, "It's about a stage manager. For pity's sake, he's part of our family."

Before I knew it, I was running. Sandal straps dug into my ankles, but I ignored constricting pain, strictly for Micha's sake.

The truck trundled along more quickly. When my feet were parallel to the back wheels, I saw something important. Micha had one of those rectangular windows, behind the driver's seat, which slide horizontally. Guess what: it was open and his ponytail flapped in the breeze. This was another subconscious signal. What else could it be? I ran harder than ever before, and then scissor kicked upward like an Olympian high jumper. I alit on the back fender, then vaulted over the tailgate. My descent was an heroic pratfall into the flatbed. The brakes screeched. I immediately got on all fours and crawled toward my friend. Our eyes met in the rearview mirror. I set both hands on the window frame, so he couldn't shut me out.

He asked rather loudly, "Are you crazy?"

"Keep driving, Micha, don't miss your appointment." He stepped on the gas pedal. My story continued: "I choose to speak of a dedicated family member, a stage manager. Deep down, you want to listen, so don't resist. The heart is a wonderful ventriloquist. My lips move, but it speaks.

"Striking the set has an emotional effect on everyone, no one more so than one man. The stage manager dabs his eyes with a polka-dot handkerchief, while he rips muslin away from the board. It is the same hanky he sneezed in, when the heat broke down. The hanky he used when mopping up a clumsy stage hand's blood. The stage manager is too sentimental to wash that hanky. Observing this burly, unshaven fellow would give you such a special feeling. For me, it is just like watching my mother."

I looked into the rearview mirror at Micha's eyes. He stared straight ahead with no expression. Oh, what a victory! The glare was gone. I, Monty Moudlyn, had conquered Micha's frown. Now his eyes were soft, and slightly wet. This was a triumphant moment in our friendship.

He said, "Monty, just get out. You don't know how I feel. You won't even listen."

"That's where you are wrong. I know exactly how you feel. Don't worry. It's always darkest before the dawn. Remember what the late Ralph Waldo Emerson said, 'The only way to have a friend, is to be one.' Well, that's why I'm here. And now, give me a smile. It's as simple as that."

"What for?"

"When I see Micha Hamilphane's precious grin, I shall leave content. It's the first step out of the bottomless pit."

Suddenly, spontaneously, and ever so wonderfully, Micha smiled so broadly that his cheeks obscured those formerly blazing eyes. It lasted a mere three seconds, and the frown returned, but it doesn't matter. My selfless crusade was successful.

Micha slowed down, allowing me to climb out. As soon as sandals met asphalt, the pickup roared away.

I wish you could have been there. Pride expanded within me, filling virtually every corner of my body. I felt as if I might explode as a result of unadulterated joy.

Thus began my destiny.

Editor's Note

Not long thereafter, Monty wrote a letter to the editor, published in newspapers throughout the Pacific Northwest.

THE HUG BRIGADE MANIFESTO

This is an open letter to the world, from Monty Moudlyn.

The Hug Brigade's stated goal is to show love to downtrodden, misunderstood gangsters, bombers, and Presidents-for-Life. All they need is a hug. Imagine how the Mideast crisis could have been averted, if just one of us had hugged PLO Chairman Arafat and said, "Yasser, I care."

We need to demonstrate interpersonal sincerity through the Platonic Embrace Paradigm. When a so-called terrorist or criminal feels the compassion of your hug, warmth of your body, and beating of your heart, he will lose his anger. We will ultimately join together, in "The Anthem of Hug Brigade":

> Off we march into the sea,
> The Hug Brigade
> We want to be free.
> We'll save the world with a hug,
> The Hug Brigade, will save you and me!

Lesson Plan

What kind of gullible twit believes in zombie outbreaks? That was what I asked people who spread those rumors. I'm a folklore professor in the Comparative Literature program at Calypso University, so I know all about the danger of mass hysteria.

I had finished my lesson plan the night before, and put two books in my satchel. I walked along the brick pathway in the Quad, between the Gothic revival buildings. Young couples held hands. Guys ran along, weighed down by backpacks bouncing sideways.

White blossoms drifted off the rows of cherry trees. Their fresh scent reminded me that some student would beg me to hold class outside.

A soprano's voice sang through the air, out of the Music Building, briefly lifting my spirits.

I trotted up the steps of Val Lewton Hall. A quick glance at the school paper brought back my annoyance. The banner headline blared: "Conway Hospital denies rumors of zombies."

The campus hospital stands just up the hill from Lewton Hall. I looked up in that direction. Several people in gowns and blue scrubs milled around outside. Maybe the staff decided to give their patients fresh air.

A bell rang in Lewton Hall. I was late again. Big deal.

The patients and employees all turned around and shuffled downhill. I wondered about that, but didn't have time to hang around. Some of my students might decide to skip class if I didn't show up in another minute or two.

I entered the building and trotted to the far end of the hallway, on the first floor.

I opened the door, walked in, set my satchel on the front table, stood behind the lectern, and gazed benignly out upon the thirty or so students.

The door opened, and a latecomer shambled in, carrying a cup of coffee. The young man didn't proffer an excuse; he just dragged his feet past me. He plopped into an open seat, swilled some coffee, and stared out the window. Most classmates were no better; they sent text messages, doodled, or napped.

Three students sat up straight, facing my direction. Two were in the front row, and one in the back of the room.

I announced, "I'm glad you made it, despite all the rumors. I was going to talk about how to transcribe interviews in your folklore assignments. Well, that's changed."

Half the students actually looked up at me.

I continued, "Today, we're going to discuss mass hysteria, like the current fad of so-called zombie outbreaks. Can someone tell us about zombies?"

A brunette named Stacy Floss raised her hand.

"They're reanimated corpses, Dr. Harris."

"Very good, Miss Floss. Do any of you know where the term zombie comes from?"

Another hand shot up. A gent named Lon Carlton sat at attention in his Army ROTC uniform.

"Sir, they come from voodoo practices in Haiti," he answered in polite tones with a Southern drawl.

"Excellent, Mr. Carlton. Tell us more. Sometimes I grow tired of the sound of my own voice."

"Voodoo priests would poison an offender, so he'd fall into a death-like coma. When the priests revived him, he'd have severe brain damage."

"You might call it a folk lobotomy," I quipped, "You're well informed, Mr. Carlton. I thought your major was military science."

"It is, sir. My parents were missionaries in Port-au-Prince. They learned all the Haitian folktales. Maybe I'll write about them for this class."

I silently thanked God for a motivated student, and commented to the group at large: "That's why I enjoy teaching folklore; I learn as much as the students."

Most of the class had gone back to doodling, texting, napping, and swilling coffee. I added, "At least I hope the students learn as much as I do."

The only other attentive student raised his hand, from the back of the room.

"Professor Harris," he asked in a tentative manner.

"Yes, Mr. Alexander?"

"Do other cultures mention zombies?"

"I'm glad you asked. As it happens, they do. Norway has a good example."

Stacy Floss chipped in, "I thought Norwegians were into trolls." I didn't respond right away, so she quickly added, "Sorry, I didn't mean to interrupt."

"It's all right, Miss Floss," I replied, "At least I know someone is listening. Norwegians called the animated, moldering corpse of a known person a *gjenganger*.

"That means an again-walker. I've noticed the new mass hysteria/popular culture slang for zombies is walkers."

Carlton raised his hand: "Sir, I don't think this reported outbreak is mass hysteria."

I smirked because disagreement also shows attentiveness. I responded, "To me, it smacks of witch hunting. Maybe it's an excuse to knock off the homeless."

I always like to look at each student individually. One of the doodlers in the front row drew a cartoon of a zombie with outstretched arms, chasing someone. The victim was a dark haired man, with large eyes, narrow cheeks, a salt-and-pepper silk sports jacket, and slacks over a stick figure frame. I almost considered it a compliment to see a caricature of me, but the context proved disturbing. Was it wishful thinking?

Stacy Floss's voice interrupted my examination of the cartoon: "What about hospital patients? I heard on the radio that some were bitten and died of a fever."

I looked back into her brown, inquiring eyes: "There you go. Mass hysteria often comes from an epidemic. The current disease is a fever, which causes coma, followed by an aggressive delirium."

She asked, "What could possibly have caused such a horrible effect?"

"I'd surmise it's a form of rabies. You've got a combination of human mad dogs afflicted with the disease, and more human mad dogs rife with murderous hysteria."

Alexander slowly raised his hand. "Professor? What do you suggest we do?"

"Get out of town." Some of the students snickered. "I'm serious. Look at the Salem Witch Trials of 1692. A few farmers had the smarts to visit relatives in Boston, until it blew over. Out of sight, out of mind. It also keeps you from getting caught up in the panic."

I was about to expound on Salem, when Alexander's halting voice interrupted my train of thought: "What if I see a walking corpse? Shouldn't I defend myself?"

"You can't shoot someone for walking funny."

"What if one of them bites me?"

"Then you can defend yourself. I'd also say you should let the wound bleed a little, then disinfect it with alcohol and peroxide."

"What about going to the doctor?"

"Sure, do that, too. Antibiotics would prevent blood poisoning."

"Sir," asked Mr. Carlton, "What if it is rabies?"

"Then you get those inoculations, through the wall of your stomach, one a day for two weeks."

Alexander ventured, "I wouldn't want that kind of shot."

As he was speaking, gunshots erupted right from the hallway. The students all looked toward our room's wooden door, which had a small window.

Carlton reacted by grabbing his satchel, whipping out a pistol and heading for the exit. I blocked him and snapped, "You could be expelled for that. What are you doing, packing a forty-five?"

"I'm not. It's a nine millimeter Beretta."

"Oh, well then that makes it all right. Wait here, Mr. Carlton, that's an order."

To his credit, he stepped back, pointed the gun down at the floor, and kept his right index finger away from the trigger.

I scrunched down, slowly turned the knob, and peeked out.

A man stood with his back to me, firing at the same crowd from near the hospital: barefoot, barelegged patients in white gowns, and employees in scrubs. Four bodies lay on the linoleum floor. I couldn't understand why the crowd didn't run the other direction.

I ducked back into the classroom and locked the door. My voice surprised me with its evenness: "We've got a mass shooting out there. I advise you to leave in an orderly manner."

Alexander asked, "Through the hall?"

"No, out the windows. We're on the ground floor. Class dismissed until further notice. I'll hold the line in here."

For once, the students listened to me. They lined up at the three fire exit windows, and piled out.

Not Carlton, though. He unlocked the door. I grabbed him by the shoulder and hissed, "What are you doing?"

"You dismissed us, sir. Barricade the door behind me."

He slung his satchel over his shoulder, then racked his pistol, opened the door, and stepped out. I locked it behind him. His broad shoulders and barrel chest made him a big target.

I didn't have time for further reflection. I piled desks in front of the door, then noticed an assistant by my side. Stacy Floss had stayed to help me with the barricade. If the term continued, I'd give her a better grade.

Shots continued ringing out. Maybe Mr. Carlton had stopped the massacre.

No such luck. Instead I saw the shooter's profile in the little window. He turned to his right and focused large green eyes on me. The knob clicked left and right, but didn't open it for him.

Stacy and I retreated across the room, toward the window. I flipped two desks on their sides, then the two of us crouched behind them.

Gunshots blew off our door's lock. The shooter pushed the door ajar, and the desks slid five inches. He poked his head in and shouted, "I'm out of ammo now. Let me in! They're not people! They're zombies. I really mean it!"

I didn't take in what he said at the time; I pieced it together later. All I knew was that an armed killer tried to break into my classroom. I heaved a desk right at him, and he stumbled backwards into the crowd of hospital employees.

They dragged him out of sight. The shooter screamed for ten seconds, then abruptly stopped.

Something else occurred to me. Had the shooter murdered my best student? I shouted, "Carlton? Carlton! Are you all right?"

The door opened and several gowned hospital patients lurched into the room. They flailed their arms and snapped their teeth.

I shouted, "I'm not with the mass killer; don't take it out on me."

I threw another desk, which collided with a patient's chest. It knocked him backwards, but he stayed on his feet. Stacy dashed over, and pepper sprayed a patient's yellow eyes. That also had no effect, so she ran back to me. More gunshots rang out, this time from behind us. A hospital patient took bullets to the chest and neck, but kept shambling toward me. I whirled around.

Mr. Carlton stood outside, aiming his pistol at the patients.

"Come on, sir, or you'll get killed."

"By you?"

"By the zombies!"

Carlton fired straight at the closest patient's forehead. A hideous arc of blood, skull fragments, and brain tissue splattered the other invaders behind the target. That person crumpled up. Carlton kept firing until all five patients lay on the floor.

More patients shuffled through the doorway. That made no sense to me. Why would they come toward the direction of the shots? None of them looked down to the carrion at their feet. Instead, they reached out in my direction. Stacy clambered out the window. I don't know why, but I still had my satchel. I hefted it out, and scrambled over the sill.

Mr. Carlton reloaded another magazine into his Beretta. Stacy and I joined him. Students ran all over the Quad, searching for friends or lovers. The reek of cordite lingered in my nostrils.

The soprano's voice still sang the aria, but her high note turned into a loud shriek.

Stacy asked me, "Did you see what happened in your classroom? Carlton shot that man in the chest and neck, but the man didn't die; not until he took a bullet in the head."

I tried to talk, but found myself hyperventilating. My breathing slowed voluntarily, and I pulled myself together. A scholar always has an answer: "Oh, I can explain that. It's related to trance-warriors, like in the Chinese Boxer Rebellion of 1900."

Alexander's voice broke in from behind me, "Will this be on the test?"

I nearly leaped out of my shoes, from being startled after all the carnage.

"Thanks for joining our mobile tutorial. I need to keep talking, or I'll go into shock."

The four of us marched away from Lewton Hall. I had no idea where to go next, and just kept lecturing:

"Trance warriors like the so-called Boxers would whip themselves into a state of high concentration. They were so hepped up on adrenaline that it often took five or six bullets to bring one of them down."

Carlton said, "Trance warriors were better organized. This is more like a feeding frenzy of sharks."

"The disease damages the mind."

"Sir, I'm not convinced that anything from history, folklore, or medicine can explain this outbreak."

"You know about the Haitian zombies."

"Not whole packs of them."

Alexander stuck his head between us. "Excuse me. Where are we going?"

For once a student had stumped me. I looked around and made a quick decision, feigning confidence: "Let's try Conway Hospital. It's the closest."

We headed up the hill, without looking back at Lewton Hall, and reached the outskirts of the large medical building. Cops in riot gear formed a perimeter. I noticed a short, uniformed woman. She had a white forelock in her black hair, and the blazing eyes of a tough street cop.

"Officer, I'm Marc Harris, visiting professor of folklore in the Comp. Lit. Department."

Carlton asked, "Who's in command, ma'am?"

She looked us all up and down, and replied, "I'm Chief Andrea Spicuzza. What can I do for you?"

I reported, "We had a mass shooting in Lewton Hall."

"What happened?"

"A man gunned down several people in the hallway, then the survivors dragged him away for frontier justice."

"Were they students or walkers?"

Carlton replied, "Definitely walkers."

"I'll keep it in mind," said the Chief. She looked back to her men.

"Keep it in mind?" I didn't bother to conceal my shock or disapproval.

"Don't you believe in enforcing the law?"

Chief Spicuzza glared straight into my face: "We are trying to maintain order in this chaos."

"Fine, can we go inside the hospital?"

"That depends, professor. Did one of those walkers bite you?"

"Not me."

Stacy shook her head. Alexander slipped his hand in his pocket, but didn't say anything. Carlton said, "No, ma'am."

Chief Spicuzza's eyes and voice softened courteously: "Then I'm sorry, you'll have to move on."

I asked, "Isn't there some place where we can make a report, or get some shelter?"

"Professor Harris," said Chief Spicuzza, "we're keeping people out of that facility. Only casualties bitten by walkers will be admitted."

Shots rang out from inside the hospital.

Alexander finally spoke: "Do you just shoot them?"

"All gunshots are in self defense," said the Chief.

I grumbled, "That's a relative term, under these circumstances."

Stacy asked, "What are we supposed to do, Chief?"

"I suggest you leave campus. We're locking it down."

Carlton stepped forward, halted, and displayed ramrod straight posture. "Pardon me, ma'am. I'm in ROTC. I can help guard the perimeter."

Much to my surprise, Chief Spicuzza smiled. "Your unit is out back. They're waiting for the National Guard."

"Are they armed, ma'am?"

"The Guard, or your unit?"

"My unit, ma'am."

"M-16s and forty-fives."

"Will you excuse us a moment, ma'am?" Carlton whispered to me, "Come over this way, sir."

Stacy, Alexander, and I followed him to behind the thick trunk of a Douglas fir. I caught sight of the Chief walking over to talk to a helmeted cop with Sergeant's stripes on his upper sleeve.

Carlton set his book bag next to the tree trunk, and unzipped it. He handed me his Beretta sideways, plus a box of bullets and couple of clips.

"Sir, I won't need this for now. My unit will provide me with weapons."

Alexander peered into the open bag and said, "Hey, you've got a first aid kit. Can we have that, too?"

"Sure, buddy. I'll have plenty of access to medical supplies in the hospital."

A simple thank you didn't seem adequate, so I said, "You'll be the first ROTC cadet to win the Medal of Honor."

Carlton grinned. "Thank you. Oh, and one more piece of advice, sir. Go to the Student Union, and stock up on whatever food and water you can find."

I holstered the pistol in my waistband, concealed by my sports jacket. I poked my head around the tree and called out, "Oh, Chief Spicuzza…?"

She stopped talking to the Sergeant and looked over in my direction.

"Yes, Professor Harris?" She mimicked the saccharine lilt in my voice.

"My two protégés and I are going to occupy the Student Union building. Any objections?"

"You have my permission."

Carlton grabbed my right hand and shook it. "Stay safe, Professor."

He picked up his bag and marched away. He saluted the Chief, she returned his salute, and he circled to the other side of the building.

Stacy and I headed side by side for the cafeteria.

I asked Stacy, "Why can't they keep delirious patients under lock and key?"

Four gunshots echoed in the distance, followed by silence.

Stacy asked, "Is this the end of the world?"

"It could take a month or two, but life will settle down." A succession of ten distant gunshots made me appear overly optimistic. Stacy Floss asked:

"Why won't you admit that Carlton was right?"

I halted: "If I do that, I'll really go nuts. How can I possibly accept predatory corpses as real?"

"You could write a book about them."

"*Community Dynamics of Zombies*: then they won't seem scary anymore. They'll become incredibly boring."

I started walking again, and she followed.

We had already lost Carlton to the call of duty. Now we had someone missing. What happened to young Brent Alexander? I stopped and looked back for him. Maybe a horde of moribund creeps had nabbed him.

Fortunately, he walked from around a bend in the path into our view. His face looked positively ashen. Alexander mopped his sweaty forehead with his hand. I didn't think about the band aid on his thumb, until much later.

Stacy asked him, "Are you okay?"

"Do you know a place where we can lie down?"

"Together?" I asked.

Stacy said, "They have couches in the Student Union. Why are you so pale?"

"Am I? Well, it's been a traumatic experience."

We reached the Student Union building, where a diminutive, middle aged janitor locked up. I said, "Excuse me, we'd like to go inside."

The janitor turned toward me. His jump suit name tag said, "Quoc Nguyen", making him Vietnamese. He answered in diction of almost exaggerated clarity: "It is closed."

"That's all right, we have permission."

"I am sorry. I cannot allow that."

"I'm a professor. My name is Marc Harris."

"No admittance is allowed. We are locking down the entire campus."

"Here's my card. Look at the driver's license. The names match."

"You have no authorization."

"The campus Police Chief told me to look after this building."

"Oh, really?" He smiled slyly and asked, "What is his name?"

"Her name is Andrea Spicuzza." The janitor didn't budge, so I pulled out another business card and a pen. I wrote on the back: "I take full responsibility for the Student Union." I signed my name and dated it, then handed it over to Quoc Nguyen, and concluded for his benefit: "This is a legal contract. Satisfied?"

I concealed my disbelief when he handed over the keys.

"Good luck, Professor Harris."

The diminutive custodian walked away, with the aplomb of the fearless.

Whether we had mass hysteria, an epidemic, or a real zombie outbreak, he could handle it. I wished he had stayed with us, but apparently he also felt the call of duty. His bosses had told him to lock down the campus, so he put obligation ahead of his safety.

I fiddled with three different keys, until one fit into the lock and opened the door.

Alexander asked, "What if other students looted the place?"

"Not likely," I replied, "Students are idealistic."

We walked down the stairway to the basement. Our footsteps echoed off the concrete floor. I unlocked the buffet room door and looked inside.

"Jackpot," I announced, "Why leave at all? Load up your bags, in case we have to make a run for it."

Alexander wheezed, "Can you load mine up for me? I've got to lie down. I noticed a nice, overstuffed couch upstairs."

He dropped his book bag on the floor and trudged away. The student used both hands to grip the steel rail, and panted while he pulled himself up. Looking back on it, I can't believe my own stupidity. He showed all early symptoms of the illness I had written off.

My foolishness is common. Professors usually know one subject, and nothing else. Take us two blocks away from a campus, and we're developmentally disabled.

Stacy and I stuffed our bags with energy bars, bottled water, bananas, apples, oranges, and muffins wrapped in cellophane. I confided, "I'm actually listening to my instincts. Let's also stock up on fire axes and knives."

Later, I loaded my tray with freshly microwaved chicken, steamed rice, and mashed potatoes. Celery and carrots, and a couple of chocolate doughnuts rounded off this epicurean feast. Stacy gave herself the same menu, since it was all that remained available. I didn't know when we'd eat another hot meal.

We sat at a table. Out of habit, I had left my satchel by my feet. It seems ridiculous now. Who was going to steal it?

We ate in silence. Besides my gun, we had an arsenal. Both of us had axes propped next to us. Sharp kitchen knives sat atop the table. Stacy scooped red sauce onto her chicken. My stomach lurched, and I clapped a hand over my mouth.

Whenever you try not to think about some horrible scene, it becomes more vivid. The shooting of those crazed patients in the classroom flooded my memory. But the worst part was the shooter, and what I had done. I put my hand down, and stared straight ahead, attempting not to remember his screams.

Stacy's voice brought me out of this waking nightmare: "Professor, you've been quiet."

That's admittedly unusual in my case. I said, "Just brooding."

"So was I. Anyone would."

"Not young Mr. Alexander. He wandered off to take a nap over two hours ago, and we haven't seen him since. It's the sleep of the guiltless."

"Maybe he's exhausted. He started flagging pretty early."

"At least he has a clear conscience. I don't know when I can sleep again."

"What do you mean?"

"I murdered an innocent man."

"Who?"

"The shooter. You were there. He was a hero, defending the classrooms. That man begged me for help, and what did I do? I threw a desk in his face. I'm responsible for those zombies ripping him apart."

"You couldn't have known that. You acted in self-defense. It's a relative term, under these circumstances."

Leave it to a psychology student to throw my words back at me. It's still annoying.

I continued, "What I did to him was bad enough. In Graduate School, they taught us that anything spreading by word-of-mouth had to be wrong. Today, I set out to prove that we had nothing to worry about, beyond rumor-driven panic."

I rifled through my bag and pulled out two books I had intended to cite in class: *Satanic Panic* by Jeffrey S. Victor, and *The Demon Haunted World* by the patron saint of agnostics, Carl Sagan.

I picked up both dog-eared paperbacks, stood and threw them across the cafeteria.

The books smashed loudly into the side of a stainless steel garbage bin, then thudded to the polished concrete floor.

Stacy asked, "What are you saying?"

"My lecture completely discredited me."

"I'm sure no one cares about today's class now."

"I put you and all of the other students in danger, by not canceling the session."

"We chose to come to your class. And you're not discredited. You're still learning, even amid all this horror."

"How?"

"Look at how adaptable you are. We've been safe in here while the campus falls apart; maybe the whole world."

I didn't have a clever comeback for that. For some reason, I rarely believe compliments.

Stacy asked, "Can I ask you a question?"

"Sure. Feel free to change the subject."

"Don't you think we should check on Brent Alexander?"

"What for?"

"What if he's infected?"

"How could that have happened?"

"Maybe he wasn't just tired. Maybe he was sick, from a bite."

"Then why wouldn't he mention it? We were right at the hospital."

"The gunshots. He must have expected the cops to shoot him, once he got behind closed doors."

I hate when the student is right. I covered my slow wittedness with smug superiority: "That's very astute, Miss Floss. Not only that, but did you notice he asked Carlton for the first aid kit?"

"That's right. I thought he was just being well prepared. And he was behind us the whole time we were walking over here."

"Because he said he was tired."

"And maybe because he didn't want us to see him taking care of a fresh bite."

"On his thumb."

She paused, and her brown eyes widened: "How did you know it was on his thumb?"

"He had a band aid on it, that's why. You've got to notice these things, Miss Floss."

"You're right, Professor. I'll try to do better." She looked down at the floor, as if I were the one who had noticed the danger first.

"Do you think he might be a zombie?" She asked.

"Maybe not."

"How do you know?"

"A monster would have barged in on us while we were eating. I've seen enough movies to know that."

I put the Beretta back in my waistband, and grabbed a fire axe with my left hand. Stacy also picked up her axe.

We tiptoed up the stairs.

Stacy whispered, "What do we do if he's a zombie?"

"Go straight for the head, the way Carlton did."

We crept up to the foyer. Night had fallen outside, but flashes of gunfire revealed Alexander's position. He stood staring out of a window, with his hands pawing at the glass. Maybe the battle excited him.

Stacy tugged on my sports jacket and whispered, "What now?"

"Maybe he's okay."

I leaned the axe against the wall, and pulled out the gun. I stopped at what I considered a safe distance, ten feet away, and asked, "Mr. Alexander? How's the view?"

Alexander turned toward me. A sustained round of gun flashes outside revealed a yellow gleam to his eyes. He gnashed his teeth, and lurched toward me.

I racked the pistol and fired twice from ten yards back. How could I have missed? At least it convinced me of his status as a zombie. A shy kid like Alexander never would have kept charging me after two bullets whizzed over his head.

I aimed more carefully and squeezed the trigger.

"I got him!" I shouted in triumph.

Technically, I did. The bullet had torn off half of his right ear.

I squeezed the trigger again, but it wouldn't move.

"Shoot him!" Stacy shrieked.

"I can't! The gun jammed!"

Stacy charged past me and behind Alexander's animated corpse. I laid the pistol on the floor and grabbed my fire axe.

Stacy sneaked up behind Alexander and swung her axe overhand, in a high arc. The blade lodged in the zombie's shoulder. Alexander wheeled around and the handle slipped from Stacy's hands, sticking out of him.

I turned my own axe around in my hands and swung it like a baseball bat, so the pointed end of the tool's head penetrated the back of Alexander's head. He lost all energy and fell limply to the floor, face forward.

I easily pulled the axe out of his skull. I stepped on the immobile corpse and grabbed the handle of Stacy's weapon. It took me three yanks to jerk the blade out of his shoulder.

I said, "We have the strength, we just need to work on our marksmanship."

"Let's see if he had a bite."

I picked up Alexander's limp right hand, and tore the band aid off his thumb. The weak light showed crescent redness from a recently scabbed wound.

I dragged what was left of a good student into the ladies' room, the nearest discreet place.

Gunshots grew steadily louder. Stacy rushed over to me, and we crouched behind the granite wall. Machine gun fire ripped the locks off the double doors. The front entrance swung open and a soldier marched in. He brandished a forty-five. The officer had Captain's bars on his visored helmet. Six soldiers armed with M-16s followed him.

The visor lifted. No, it wasn't a woman.

"Mr. Carlton," I called out, "It's me, Dr. Harris."

"Who's with you, sir?"

"Me, Stacy Floss."

Carlton walked toward us. "Where's Brent Alexander?"

I pointed to the ladies' room. "We lost him, and not from rabies." I picked up the Beretta by the barrel, and handed it over. "Here's your pistol. It jammed."

Carlton pulled out the clip, racked the pistol, and the jammed bullet flew out. He reloaded the gun and handed it back to me. Then he asked, "Is the commissary intact?"

"All except for what we ate."

Carlton pointed to two enlisted men and ordered, "You two stand guard."

I asked him, "Well, Captain Carlton, how did you know we'd still be here?"

He handed me my business card, with my note and signature on it.

Carlton explained, "A janitor named Quoc Nguyen gave it to me. ROTC cadets have been ordered to the nearest fort. We want to stock up on food and water first. Will you come with us, sir?"

"Gladly," I replied, "I might learn something useful."

Roscoe Gat

Treason against the United States shall consist only in levying War against them, or in adhering to their Enemies, giving them Aid and Comfort. No person shall be convicted of Treason unless on the Testimony of two Witnesses to the same overt Act, or on confession in open Court.

United States Constitution, Article III, Section 3

No one believes me. It's strange that I used to suffer from a combination of depression and fear, like a weight pressing down on my shoulders and head. Yet now, I have no qualms in writing about what befell me.

I'm not crazy. A madman hears voices. Some people have mistaken, or misdiagnosed me, for mentally ill because of my talent for making connections. I'm also highly observant.

It was a typically raw November evening on Seattle's Fifth Avenue. Lights from clothing stores lit up the otherwise grim, drizzly darkness. Heavy mist sheeted down. That kind of precipitation is light enough so that any breeze wafts the droplets around, soaking you thoroughly, even if you have an umbrella. I did, but I'd held the bumbershoot up so long that my right bicep ached. Rivulets ran down the left sleeve of my brown leather jacket. Not only that, but my jeans pant legs had become damp and clammy, from the thighs down to the ankles.

I stiffened up and looked over my shoulder at the middle aged woman in a tan camel coat. She had short, spiky hair, and wore big glasses like from the 1970s. Her styles were wrong, like a bad disguise.

I looked to the front, then swiveled my head and locked eyes on her. Sure enough, I caught her looking at me. What was her game? Push me in front of a bus? Stab me with a hypodermic? Their assassins were smooth, all right.

I could have fought it out with my weapon, but that would attract attention. It would be more discreet to slip away.

Most Seattleites don't jaywalk. I broke the tradition and dashed across the slick street, heading north, twenty feet beneath the monorail. A Mercedes skidded, but I dodged past its fender. Then I made it to the sidewalk. A little old lady yelled up, "You're not supposed to do that."

I ignored the scold, turned left, and double-timed all the way around the three-sided building. I looked back around my shoulder, but the camel coat lady had not pursued me. This confirmed the success of my escape.

Still I needed to slip in somewhere plausible, and remain inconspicuous. This is not easy when you stand six-foot-six. That's when I entered my favorite clothing store. A gust of warm air greeted me when the automatic doors slid open, and I stepped in.

Two salespeople loitered at the cash register, to the left of the entrance. Why do small, skinny people work in shops like this?

I tilted my head down toward a man in a pinstripe suit. He beamed, "Hello, sir, welcome to Utica Big & Tall. I'm Barron Dailey. How can I help you?"

"Oh, I just wanted to go downstairs and check out some products there."

"Sure, right down this way to the bargain basement." He held out a copper receptacle and said, "This is an umbrella stand." I took the hint, and deposited my dripping bumbershoot.

He led me around a big cabinet behind the cash register, then around a square wooden pillar. We trod down a carpeted staircase. I counted forty steps in all, including the landing in the middle.

Racks of clothes hung all around me, providing extra shelter. I'd need it. I looked around for the green sign saying, EXIT, just in case anyone followed me.

Barron explained about the various items shipped from Frisco, Vegas, and Beverly Hills. He pointed to the racks of shirts, and said, "Those are the tall sizes. We put them up there, so the sleeves and shirt tails won't sweep the floor."

Could I trust this man? I doubted it.

His spiel continued. I nodded along, as if listening. Maybe the conspiracy trained him well. You can tell if someone is a member because of their robotic memorization of cover stories.

But then, Barron Dailey surprised me by relating on a more human level.

"I've never seen so many giants in my life as when I started working here. I'm talking about men who stand seven feet tall."

"Really? Who was the tallest?"

"Some retired basketball player. He must have been seven foot two."

"He'd make me feel short."

"I feel like a dwarf in here. Speaking of giants, my father once saw the tallest man in the world, Robert Wadlow."

"When was that?"

"In Portland, in the 1930s."

I flinched. Portland is a hotbed of the conspiracy. Barron continued, "Wadlow was as tall as a lamppost. He toured the country as a gimmick for a footwear company, because he wore size thirty-six. He stood eight feet, eleven inches tall."

"Maybe you guys need someone like that in your catalogues."

"I know. I'm sick of a big and tall company's catalogues showing these little pretty boys. We ought to hire big, beefy football players, or opera singers."

This was not your typical salesman. They usually worship the companies they shill for. I said, "How come your corporation doesn't advertise? I didn't even know this place was here, the last time I shopped. I just happened to walk into it."

"I did a demo for a radio commercial, but the company wouldn't run it."

"You did? How did it go?"

"Well, first this heroic music plays." He called up the stairs, "Hey, Julie."

The petite, middle aged brunette looked down to us.

"Give him the opening of our commercial."

She took three dainty steps down the staircase, and then boomed out, "And there came from the camp of the Philistines, a champion named Goliath, whose height was six cubits and a span. He had a helmet of bronze on his head, and he was armed with a coat of mail…"

Barron enthused, "Then the music turns to rock and roll, and a man's voice says, 'Today, Goliath would shop at Utica Big & Tall in Seattle.' Then the announcer describes the great products here. The whole commercial lasts a minute."

I smiled. These two had quoted the Bible, so they couldn't be part of the conspiracy. The small woman looked toward the door and stepped away.

Apparently Barron enjoyed talking, because he regaled me with the story of the fattest man in the world. Barron said he had heard legends on Bainbridge Island, thirty years earlier in the late 1970s, of a nine hundred pound man who owned a taxi company. John Minnoch drove the cab literally from the back seat, because that was the only way he could fit inside. But, Barron explained, the legends weren't true. Minnoch actually weighed 1400 pounds. The shockingly obese cabby held two *Guinness Book of World Records* entries: heaviest man, and biggest weight difference in a marriage.

Barron must have been older than he looked, to remember the 1970s. Judging by the pallor of his skin, I'd say he avoided sunshine.

Barron and I talked a little more, and I deemed him trustworthy. That's when I opened up: "My relatives have been cheating me."

"They have?"

"Yes. First they got my grandmother to disinherit me. They put a new will in front of her and made her sign it, taking all my money for themselves."

"I'm sorry to hear that."

"But they wouldn't stop there. They tried to kill me."

"Did you call the police?"

"No, I couldn't, because they used the perfect murder weapon. I was lying down in a bedroom. They stacked up forty microwave ovens on the other side of the wall. Then they turned on the ovens at full blast, to try to kill me."

"Did you see them do this?"

"No, I told you, I was in the room alone."

"Then how do you know the did that?"

"Simple. I heard them stack up the ovens. After the machines all beeped on at once, the whirring commenced. My relatives all ran out at once. I tried to get out of the room, but the door was stuck. Then I tried to open the window, but my relatives had obviously painted it shut. I pounded on the glass, yelling for passersby: 'Let me out! Let me out!'

"That's when my relatives turned off the ovens, and hid them. I finally ripped the hinges out of the door and escaped the room. By that time, the ovens were gone. Pretty slick, weren't they?"

He didn't say anything after that. The report of my relatives' evil actions left Barron thunderstruck. He probably didn't realize anyone could be that sinister.

I continued: "It turns out my relatives are part of the Inter-Municipal Neo-Pagan Conspiracy. It includes the Multnomah County Sheriff's Department in Oregon. Some of my relatives are celebrities, like Sammy Hagar and Joan Jett."

"The rock stars? And they want your mother's money."

"My grandmother's money," I corrected him. He probably tested me to make sure I didn't change my story. "That's why they're so rich. But I'm onto them. I'm writing a book-length expose to blow the lid off the conspiracy."

After a long pause, Barron looked up the staircase and said, "Oh, I'm sorry, the Assistant Manager wants me."

I looked up the stairs and said, "I don't see her there."

"She signaled to me, and then walked to the front of the store. She needs my help. Sorry, but I can't keep her waiting."

He walked up the stairs and didn't look back to me.

That's just as well. Maybe I could hide in a fitting room until the heat wore off.

On the other hand, I might want to listen in.

I tiptoed up the forty carpeted steps, tuned my ears, and peered over the long cabinet. They had their backs to it; they faced toward the cash registers and doors to the right of the cash wrap desk. Julie told Barron to pass her a roll of quarters. He obeyed. Their fingertips met for less than a second, which caused Julie to whip her hand away from Barron, as if she had touched a hot kettle.

To my relief, their chores had nothing to do with me. I walked back downstairs.

I listened to the piped in music, because it might have a message for me. If the place had songs sung by my relatives, then I was in trouble. The two salespeople might call the authorities. Other victims of the conspiracy occasionally put songs with coded messages in the music played on radio stations, waiting rooms, and in elevators. I'm not some kind of nut, who thinks he gets messages from the TV. That's just plain absurd.

I listened to so many songs that my jeans had turned light blue again. The moisture had evaporated. Perhaps Julie & Barron had forgotten about me. I sneaked back up and resumed my surreptitious observations. the key to camouflage is to remain immobile. And that's when I got a surprise.

It isn't every day one sees a celebrity. A corpulent man held court with the two salespeople. Barron glared at him sideways, from a distance of ten feet. Julie showed the man some huge shirts.

Their customer was Mickey Mondo, the movie maven. It's hard not to recognize a vain fat man. He was so in love with himself that he had a three-day beard growth on his sloppy fat jowls. He wore a baseball cap, even indoors, and his porcine eyes squinted at you from black rimmed, square glasses. He waddled around in size 54 jeans and a quadruple extra large, all-weather jacket.

I had seen his alleged documentaries, too. People have the gall to call me crazy. Mondo always adhered to Enemies of the United States, making his movies about how wonderful it was to live under a totalitarian system, or serve in a terrorist's un-uniformed army. His movies also mocked Christians and Jews, while lauding every other religion. He won an Oscar for a feature length documentary about a prison cult that worshiped old Norse gods. The "hero" of his movie was an inmate who had led a failed jail break at the Rawlins State Pen in Wyoming, after the gang had bludgeoned a corrections officer to death. Mondo touted the killing as a First Amendment, freedom of religion issue.

The latter movie had convinced me of Mondo's involvement with my relatives in the Inter-Municipal Neo-Pagan Conspiracy.

And so, Mickey Mondo held forth to the employees. He preached with a big grin on his doughy face. Higher up on his cheeks was the pitting on his skin from having gorged on too many fats. He told Barron & Julie their prices were too high, they didn't have enough products, and they were "running dogs" of corporate fat cats. I imagine this was his way of haggling.

When Julie showed him a less expensive shirt, Mondo looked at the label. "Ha," he snorted, "Made in Bangladesh. Our Zionist Occupied Government let your cartel outsource the job to little children in sweat shops. When will your company stop using child labor?"

Julie replied, "I don't think they do."

"You're a collaborator in slavery. When will you make it stop?"

"That's not my decision."

"Oh, so you admit your corporation exploits kids at poverty wages."

Barron said, "She didn't admit anything of the kind."

"That means she's concealing it."

"We just sell the products, sir."

Mickey Mondo held forth some more: if they wanted his business, they'd better clean up their corrupt act. Everyone who worked for Utica Big & Tall was complicit in the savage exploitation of innocent Muslim children: "Now, what are you going to do about it?"

Julie responded, "I'll pray for them."

Mondo guffawed.

The automatic door slid open and a long armed, lanky man ducked in. Julie trotted over to speak to him.

Barron said to Mickey Mondo, "I'd suggest you look at some of our bargains downstairs. I need to scrub the toilet."

Barron must have been the best dressed janitor on the West Coast.

This cued me to slink downstairs. Then I padded to the nearest fitting room, and stepped inside. I reached under my left arm and gripped the heel of an icy weapon.

Elephantine footsteps plodded down the stairs. The floor vibrated when he walked on it. I looked down from over the fitting room door at him, in profile. The great director curled his upper lip at the merchandise.

The fitting room door squeaked open. The director slowly turned around in my direction. I said in my best, eerie delivery, "So, Mister Mondo, we meet at last."

"I hope you're a fan."

"A relative, as if you didn't know."

"Can't say that I did." He looked at me with knotted eyebrows, as if trying to recognize my face, "You look familiar."

I closed in on him, with my hand still gripping the concealed object of power.

"Do you know what?" He said, "I know why you look familiar. I saw a face like yours in North Korea."

That stopped me in my tracks. How was that possible? He said, "Sure, they have posters of a jackboot crushing a blond haired, blue eyed man with a big nose and jutting chin. Not only that, but you're tall. You look like the Ugly American to those good people." He chuckled merrily. "So, relative, what's your name?"

"You know my name."

"Okay," he said slowly and carefully, but still grinning, "please tell me your name."

I pulled out my .357 magnum and stuck it to his temple, "Call me Roscoe Gat."

"Hey, wait a minute, buddy. I don't believe in guns."

"Do you want to find out if it's real or not?"

"Take it easy." His voice shook.

"Right, Mondo. We'll take it easy together."

"What'll you do if I yell for help?"

"I'll blow your fat face off. Then I'll pump lead into your belly. It'll be the most nutritious meal you've eaten in years."

"What do you want? Money, right?"

"I wanted my grandmother's legacy, but you and the others cheated me out of it."

"No, I didn't"

"Are you contradicting me?" I stuck the gun right between his eyes.

"Yes, I mean no. I mean, I don't know what you mean."

"You're not making sense. You're a crazy man. You and I are going to take a trip together."

"Are we going out the emergency exit down here?"

Had he read my mind? No, it was actually a logical question. That had been Plan A, but I'm quick on my feet: "Why do you want to go out the basement?"

"I just assumed…"

"You just assumed that we'd go out that way and an alarm bell would ring. You just assumed that the clerks upstairs would get suspicious, and start looking for us. You just assumed you'd drop your wallet and a note behind."

"Come on, I never did anything to you."

"Yes you did. Stop contradicting me."

The gun barrel slid down the bridge of his sweating nose. He gasped. His unshaven jowls quivered. The stubble stood straight up.

I said, "I'll tell you what we're going to do, cousin. We're going to walk up those stairs, and you aren't going to make a sound. We'll say goodbye to the clerks together. Now walk."

He climbed the stairs ahead of me. He stopped and panted on the landing. "Keep going," I ordered.

"Let me catch my breath." His chest heaved, and he doubled over.

"Come on," I snapped, "I'm in a hurry."

He hyperventilated in time to the muzak. I nudged him to move on. He looked down at the gun. I pointed it up at his face. That would make it look as big as a cannon.

This was self-defense. If I had him as my hostage, then the rock stars would give back my money, and end their reign of terror.

"Keep going," I prodded him.

Now his side fat shook, making his jacket tremor. He hesitated and I pushed him.

We came up behind the long cabinet and the pillar, to our right. I said, "Hold it. Here's what we're going to do. I'm going to conceal my pistol under my coat. It'll be pointing straight at you. If you make one noise or gesture to give me away, I'll shoot your belly twice. Then I'll shoot your thighs. And I'll save the last two shots for your wrists. Do you know what'll happen then? You'll bleed to death, in searing agony. Won't that be fun?"

"We can forget this whole thing. I'll do anything you want."

"You'll be my hostage, when we call the other relatives."

Julie greeted a customer. I whispered, "Stay here on the stairs and don't make a move. Get it?"

"Yes."

I peered over the cabinet, like a Kilroy graffito. An average sized man in a green, canvas jacket had wandered in. Julie inquired, "Hello, sir. What brings you in today?"

"You should know. You're sending me brain waves to come in here."

The young man ambled over to a set of shelves, covered by crisply folded stacks of polo shirts, arranged by size and color. Quintuple Extra Large formed a wide base at the bottom, while other shirt sizes pyramided their way up to the just plain Large. The solidly colored stacks included reds, blues, whites, forest greens, yellowish greens, purple, almost every color imaginable.

The young man in the canvas jacket and jeans gazed upon the colorful stacks. He swayed side to side. His hair looked like it had dew drops on it, from that misty rain outside.

I had him pegged as a space cadet, flying on hallucinogens. I can't stand people like that. Aren't there enough mentally ill patients without bums who pay money to put themselves in an altered state of consciousness? Illegal drug users are parasites. I would have shot him, but my gun wasn't actually loaded.

The young man then shuffled over to a rolling rack near the cash register. It had row after row of multi-colored silk shirts.

Julie & Barron didn't interact with him. They folded pants or totted up figures. Then Barron did something unexpected. He walked to the front door and propped it open. Cars roared by.

The druggie looked out the door, and swept himself outside. Barron allowed the doors to glide shut again.

Julie asked Barron, "What did you do that for?"

"He had the brains of a moth, so I figured he'd follow the headlights of the cars going by."

"Good thinking."

"Maybe you'll see him on your way to the bus stop."

She mumbled something.

"What did you say?"

"I was praying."

"For him?"

"No, for the children in the Third World factories.

I shooed Mondo back downstairs. I had changed my mind, deciding that I didn't want him to signal the workers. They were properly distracted, but too close together. I needed them separated.

Mondo plumped down on the carpeted staircase.

"On your feet," I growled.

"Can't I sit down?"

"Not yet, Mondo. You'll have plenty of time to sit down later."

He took off his ubiquitous baseball cap and ran the back of his sleeve over his wet forehead. His sideburns were sopping from perspiration. When was the last time this jerk had exercised? Maybe it was when he got out of a chair and walked up the few steps, on his way to the podium to accept an Oscar.

Mondo's sweat emitted pungent musk. It probably arose from perspiration gathering in rolls of avoirdupois. He asked, "Can't we talk about this?"

"Not till we're in the proper place. You'll call your agent, and he'll gather the extended family. That's when we'll talk."

"Ransom?"

"Not ransom. Reclamation. I was disinherited because of your conspiracy. You and our relatives will give back what's rightfully mine."

We trudged back up the stairs. From the way he panted, you'd think we scaled Mount Everest. I stopped him again and eavesdropped.

Didn't those damn clerks have anything to do? Change some light bulbs, for God's sake, I thought. What happened to that giant who had come in a while ago?

Barron said to Julie, "Well, you made a good sale today, at last. One of us has to check on those guys downstairs. I nominate you."

"That's unusually generous. Don't you want the commission?"

"I don't want to deal with that nut again."

It was unkind of him to refer to Mondo that way.

Car brakes screeched outside, followed by a loud thump. Barron said, "That sounded bad. The streets are slick. I hope no one got hurt."

Julie replied, "I'll say a prayer. Meanwhile, we need to make more sales. Do you want to wait on Mr. Mondo?"

"I've seen his films. He's a traitor, a radical, and a heretic."

Talk about escalation. Now I knew Barron didn't belong to the conspiracy. Good on him!

Julie mumbled to herself.

Barron asked, "What are you doing?"

"I'm praying for Mr. Mondo."

"That's a wasted effort. Did you see Mondo's documentary, which touted North Korea as a workers' paradise? Or how about his pagan documentary in favor of that murderer in Wyoming? Then when Mondo made it to the microphone at the Oscars, he denounced the War against Al-Qaeda as a witch hunt by President Obama. I'll never forgive him for any of that."

"You have to forgive him."

"No, I don't."

"It's important for your soul."

"Okay, I'll forgive him when he dies."

I whispered to Mondo, "Do you hear that? He's on my side."

Julie snapped at Barron, "And you call yourself a Christian."

"Do you know what my favorite movie title is? *God Forgives, I Don't*."

"That's terrible."

"It was a terrible movie, but a great title. It sums up my philosophy of life."

"How can you not forgive people?"

"It's permission for them to do more rotten things."

"If you forgive them, they'll become better people."

"No, they don't. They take advantage of you."

Apparently this theological debate would drag on for a while, so I nudged Mondo and pointed down to the basement.

"Not again," he whined.

Down we trod. Julie & Barron's bickering continued above us. I mulled over Julie's revulsion at human contact with Barron, and the way they sniped at each other. You'd think they were married.

It finally occurred to me how to separate the two of them.

I shouted up, "Oh, Miss Julie…"

She poked her head around the pillar and said, "Yes, sir?"

"She'll protect me," said Mondo, almost to himself.

I ignored him, "I was wondering about what's on sale down here."

Sirens blared.

Julie turned away from us. I heard Barron exclaim to her, "It's worse than I expected out there. I'll be right back."

I fixed Mondo a glare. "Did you alert the authorities?"

"No."

"Of course you'd deny it," I said.

"How could I inform them?"

"The Inter-Municipal Neo-Pagan Conspiracy has its methods."

"The what?"

"Don't play ignorant with me. Now move it up those stairs. We're just going to push past them in the confusion. Barron is on my side."

"Baron who? Some English nobleman?"

"Is that supposed to be funny? Barron is the name of the salesman upstairs, as if you care. He's the one who cursed your name. You made a point of getting on his bad side with your taunting. Do you think he'll help you now? Barron and I have excellent rapport. He understands the conspiracy. Now get a move on!"

"How did you get a gun?" He stalled.

"I saved up for it. You, Sammy Hagar, Joan Jett, and the others stole Grandma's money, but I had some of my own left over."

"How did you get a permit?"

"I don't have a criminal record. You should know. The family had me committed for observation for three days; that's not a felony. The law is on my side."

I prodded Mondo with the magnum again, and he dragged himself up the stairs. He looked back at me. His face went from ashen to gray. I pushed his back: "Up! Up!"

He wasn't merely panting any more, but seriously wheezing and hyperventilating. The heavy breathing soon took on a strange rattle.

Voices were raised upstairs. What could be going on? Had the conspirators caught up with me?

I pushed past Mondo and ordered him to stay put. Then I took a good look. Terror rushed from my heart. My skin chilled from adrenalin-driven horror. I stifled a gasp.

A uniformed policeman and a young brunette stood by the cash register.

Her eyes were puffy and red. The girl's legs trembled under her raincoat.

Mine did, too. Of all the bad luck. How did this happen? I holstered my gun, and admitted defeat.

"Your friends are here," I said to Mondo, "It's a policeman."

"Officer!" Mondo shouted. He swung upward and his right fist collided with my chin. It stung.

Mondo bolted past me: "Officer!"

His glasses fell off. Mondo's chest heaved and he grabbed his left arm. His eyes bulged. He staggered back and collapsed sideways like a falling wall of bricks, then his inert body oozed down the stairs, one step at a time until he rested face down on the landing. His arms had become pinned under his chest. Mondo's legs spread akimbo, at right angles at the knees, on the stairs.

Mission aborted. I had lost my hostage. Perhaps I could bluff my way past the policeman.

Sure enough, the officer dashed around the pillar, "My God, what happened here?"

"I don't know, sir, he just collapsed."

I stepped discreetly around the pillar. The cop took a radio mike off his shoulder and spoke into it.

I came around the corner, where Julie massaged the shoulders of the young woman with the tear-streaked face.

Julie said, "God sent you in here."

"Why's that?" sobbed the girl.

"Because we can prove the accident wasn't your fault."

"God didn't send her to this shop," Barron corrected archly, "I ran out and saw the body in front of the car. Then I convinced the cop to bring her in here so we could corroborate her story about the accident."

I asked Barron, "Accident? What's going on? Who sent the police here?"

"Oh," said the salesman, "I guess you didn't know. We had a guy in the shop who was high on some psychedelic drug. I opened the door and he left. This young lady hit him with her car when he stood out in the street. Julie and I assured the cop that the victim was definitely acting strangely when he came in here."

"You know what? I saw him, too. He wasn't rational, like us."

Julie mumbled prayers.

Barron looked around and asked, "What happened to the patrolman?"

"It's weird," I said, "It looks like you lost a customer."

Barron stepped around the pillar and called down to the cop, "What happened?"

"Cardiac arrest," said the policeman. The officer had rolled Mondo onto his back and attempted CPR.

Barron rushed down the stairs and offered to perform mouth-to-mouth resuscitation. That was a gallant, yet futile gesture. I figured the Valkyries had already carried Mickey Mondo to Valhalla. After all, he died courageously in battle against me.

Julie comforted the girl: "Did you hear what the officer said? We'll testify at the inquest. It wasn't your fault."

That was right. A hallucinating fool had tripped out in front of the headlights of a moving vehicle. It was an accident.

Not so with Mondo. That was a clear case of self-defense. His involvement in the conspiracy had left me destitute. Our relatives had attempted to zap me with the microwaves. The spiky haired woman in the camel coat stalked me. And then Mickey Mondo had arrived, to silence me for good.

But I won't be silent any more. I'm no longer afraid. Power had switched to my favor. This would send a message to my relatives, not to mess with me.

To show my good will, I purchased a couple of shirts. I said to Julie, "Barron was helping me. Make sure you credit him for the sale."

She put the shirts in a paper Utica Big & Tall shopping bag, then covered them with tissue paper. I scooped up my umbrella out of the copper stand, thanked her, and trotted out.

Rain had stopped. Frigid wind cut like a knife down my neck and into my chest. I pulled my collar tight and walked away. I marched southbound, past the cops' yellow tape around the girl's station wagon. A patrolman snapped flash pictures. A red ambulance stood waiting, with the engine turned off. The druggie's body resembled a fallen mannequin display for casual clothing.

I continued walking. Cars trundled by, but I didn't look at their headlights.

A Janitor's Territory

The acridness of ammonia filled the hallway. Don Mullen, high school custodian, rested his mop handle against a row of lockers. Fluorescent tubes hummed in the ceiling, and their weak light reflected off his pate. He turned around and pushed the horizontal bar that opened the steel, blue door, then flipped down the metal door stopper. Cool autumn air wafted in, along with a teacher, Mr. Fey.

The instructor held his head back, and posed in his Navy blazer and charcoal gray slacks. "Hi, Don."

Mullen ignored the greeting and glared into the rhododendrons by the foot path. An orange tabby covered up a little hole. "Dangnabbit," roared Mullen, in an Appalachian twang. "I hate cats! Go on! Shoo!"

The tabby cocked its head at him, with an air of mild interest, and ambled around a corner.

Mr. Fey commented, "This is interesting. Are you ailurophobic?"

"Am I what? I don't understand two dollar words."

"It means you have an overwhelming fear or hatred of cats."

Mullen's boots scuffed along the checkerboard pattern of black and white tiles. He picked up the mop, dipped it in ammonia-laced water, and slopped it onto the floor.

"Sorry to spoil your chipper mood, Mr. Fey, but I just can't stand felines in my area."

Mr. Fey nodded, even though Mullen didn't look up to him.

A loud voice from across the schoolyard made them jerk their heads up: "There is no I in *team!*"

Thirty yards away, Coach Gordon Prince leaped around on the lawn. The hood of his sweatshirt and the whistle, around his bull neck, bounced freely. He had ambushed a youth in a football jersey and a girl in a cheerleader uniform. Coach Prince stopped jumping long enough to launch into an exhortation worthy of King Henry V at the Battle of Agincourt: "I learned team spirit in the Corps. You'll learn it on the football field of honor. Now drop to the grass and give me twenty push ups!"

The football player looked at the cheerleader, nodded to her, and pointed both of his open palms down toward the lawn.

The coach bellowed, "Not her; you!"

The athlete obeyed and performed the physical task. The stocky coach continued: "Psych out your opponent! Psych them out! There is no I in *team*, but there are two I's in *team spirit*. I've got both my eyes on you. You've got the hustle, you've got the drive, you've got the endurance. We will triumph as Olympic League champions!"

Mr. Fey said to Don Mullen, "Coach Gordon Prince is a fascinating case study in Post Traumatic Stress Disorder, from the Marines."

"In my day, we called it combat fatigue," said Mullen, "Where'd he get it? I-Rack? Afghanistan?"

"San Diego. He lost his mind in boot camp."

"How can you tell?"

Mr. Fey explained, as if reading the citation for the Silver Star: "Prince jumped on a grenade simulator, using his helmet to contain the blast. Then, despite painful burns, he attacked a tank with an unloaded rifle and bayonet. He seriously believed the base was under enemy attack. Coach Prince's Congressman bumped up the psychiatric discharge to an Honorable Discharge."

"Mr. Prince sure is gung-ho."

"That's great for a P.E. teacher. Too bad he also teaches chemistry."

"How do you know all this, Mr. Fey?"

"He told me, in private."

"You teach psychology. Aren't you supposed to keep your mouth shut?"

"Oh, I'm not a therapist, so I can gossip as much as I like."

Mr. Fey elbowed Don Mullen in the ribs and winked. The janitor glared at him sideways, then rolled his eyes. Both men stopped watching the football coach, now running in place, and returned to the hall. Mr. Mullen put his head down, picked up the implement, and mopped the floor.

Mr. Fey asked, "Were you in the service, Don?"

"Yes. I spent ten years in the Navy, till my Medical Discharge. I was Master-at-Arms on a big old flat-top, the *USS Nimitz*. Now what am I doing? Swabbing the deck while some know-it-all college boy loves himself in front of a bunch of dumb kids."

"Let's not be too hard on our Coach Prince."

"I didn't mean him."

"That's all right, you don't need to point out any of my colleagues by name." Mr. Fey smirked to himself, not noticing the awkward pause that ensued. Don Mullen's mop squished back and forth.

Mr. Fey changed the subject rather abruptly, "Say, Don, you should have heard the lively discussion in one of my classes. It relates to you and cats." He paused, as if waiting for the custodian to ask about the classroom conversation. Mr. Fey continued, "We discussed hatred and fear. One of my students said you hate what you fear becoming. Then I said," with extended emphasis on the first-person pronoun, "that I was afraid of bears, but didn't expect to turn into one. That got a laugh."

Don Mullen splashed his mop back into the bucket.

Mr. Fey prosed on: "I pointed out that experience is the best teacher. That's what often leads to fear and hatreds. I'll know I've reached the students if they start calling me *Mister Experience*. Do you know why? It would mean I was their best teacher."

That boast nauseated the janitor more than ammonia stench. Mullen gave a sidelong glance at the beaming instructor. The custodian knew students really called their psych teacher *Mister Smug*.

"So, Don, let's get back to you and your fear of felines. Have you had bad experiences with cats? Did your family have a nasty tom who mauled the Louis XIV chair cushions, clawed the curtains, or nibbled up the caviar?"

"No! My pappy hated cats and I don't like them neither."

The next awkward pause effectively concluded the conversation. Still, Mr. Fey found a way to have the last word: "I understand." Mr. Fey gave Don a reassuring pat on the shoulder. The janitor grimaced. "Your father taught you to hate them. The class will find that very interesting tomorrow."

Don stopped mopping. Yes, Mr. Fey could gossip as much as he liked. The teacher said, "I'll leave you to your work, Don. Have fun."

Mr. Fey stepped gingerly along the baseboard, with his black wingtip shoes avoiding sections just mopped by the janitor.

Coach Prince's voice resounded from outside, "Now do your homework, for the team!"

Mullen carried on with the chore. The youth in the Varsity football jersey and the cheerleader held hands and walked past him, their tennis shoes squeaking. The boy must have been a senior, and at least a head taller than the girl. The little cheerleader gazed adoringly up past the boy's broken nose, and into his squinting eyes.

Mullen boiled with resentment and thought, "Why should a loser like that foot-brawler have such a great looking gal? I never had a pretty girlyfriend."

The custodian politely remonstrated, "Hey! I don't like it when you kids track on this here floor, right after I mopped it!"

The couple halted, then looked behind them. Their footprints on the tiles resembled those of a father and child.

The boy said flatly, "Sorry, Mr. Mullins."

The cheerleader added, "It won't happen again."

"You're darn right it won't, or your next date will be vacuuming the teachers' lounge." The last word in the sentence took on two syllables, and sounded like *la-yoonge*. He muttered audibly to himself, "Dumb jock can't even get my name right."

The football player whispered, "Babe, I thought his name was Mullins."

"No, honey," she corrected in gentle tones, "It's Mullen."

"Shouldn't he have a name tag on his jump suit?"

"Let's just go. I don't think he wants us here."

Don Mullen snarled back, "You catch on fast."

The athlete asked the cheerleader, "What did he mean by that?"

"I'll explain it later," she replied.

They hurried around the corner.

Mullen's green eyes glared out of deep sockets. He knew what students said about him, when they thought he wasn't around. He didn't care about the opinions of these two, since he'd already brought them down to his level. Still, he wondered what Mr. Fey would brag about next.

Mullen picked up the bucket, lugged it into the men's room, and dumped the contents into a toilet. He flushed it, then set the bucket and mop in a closet. Mullen plodded back through the hall, since that part of the floor had dried now. He glanced with satisfaction at his reflection in the black tiles, while sparkling white tiles reflected glowing fluorescent tubes in the ceiling.

The custodian stepped outside and looked around. He sneaked behind the rhododendrons, knelt, and put his hands on leafy topsoil.

His body shrank while short, black fur sprouted from his skin. Ears extended upwards in a triangular manner. Hands transformed into paws. His body had shrunk, so he wriggled out of his blue jumpsuit.

Meanwhile, Coach Prince dashed back into the schoolyard and shouted to the open space, as if roaring to a stadium crowd, "Go, team! Psych them out!"

Don Mullen, in the form of a cat, thought in a human voice, "That's what I aim to do, Coach."

The ebony feline twitched his tail and slinked toward the open window of the teacher's lounge. What were they saying about him today? Fresh claw marks on wool slacks would give that gossipy psych teacher a whole new phobia.

My Script Is M*U*D

Cast of Characters

BENNY DORIAN is a tall, fair haired, blue eyed indie film director. He will read the scene descriptions of his new script. He wears a baseball cap with the title *M*U*D*, on it.

ADONIS NORTH is an amateur theatrical director, of about sixty years in age, with a shaved head, and rasping tobacco & whiskey scarred voice.

MR. MacKAY works as a drama teacher and occasional actor, and shall read the part of "The Killer." He is in his mid-fifties, with styled hair, a moustache, and deep tan. He wears a yellow suit and a gaudy neck tie. The gent speaks in a suave manner.

MARY DITTMAN, an ancient costumer, will read the role of "Jill Crown." Mary dresses respectably and hobbles around with a walker. She has a creaky voice.

MARCO WRIGHT, a corpulent character actor, will read the part of "Johnny Crown." He wheezes frequently.

RANDALL LORD, a young barista, finds himself cast as "Jack Crown." He is in his late teens, always wears a wool cap, ripped jeans, and sweater.

This play's first performance took place at the Winslow Arms, Bainbridge Island, Washington, on November 12, 2012. It later ran as a pod cast on the following website: www.jasonmarcharris.com

Troupes are allowed to perform this play free of charge in amateur settings, as long as they report their performances to the author, via the above website. The troupe must also give credit to this book.

Daytime in a dilapidated building in the Belltown neighborhood of Seattle, winter of 2012. Short, bald ADONIS NORTH talks with tall, blue eyed, blond Nordic man, BENNY DORIAN. Benny wears a baseball cap that says M*U*D. He also wears a windbreaker, flannel shirt, and jeans. These are the hackneyed accoutrements of a movie maker. A video camera stands on a tripod, facing a long boardroom table with folding chairs.

ADONIS [*raspy, tobacco-scarred voice*]: It's freezing in here. I can see my breath in the draft. Is this how you visualized your career after film school?

BENNY: Of course.

ADONIS: Hosting a script reading in a condemned building?

BENNY: Come on, Adonis. It's not condemned. It's being remodeled.

ADONIS: Don't defend the building, Benny. You've directed two independent movies. You should come up with a better venue for a screenplay reading.

BENNY: One of my movies won the Audience Award at the Melbourne Independent Filmmakers Festival.

ADONIS: Really? In Australia?

BENNY: No, in Florida. That's okay; I like to let people assume it was overseas.

ADONIS [*cautioning/doubting tone*] Independent movies are money pits. Do you really think you can raise five million bucks for this project?

BENNY: Of course, Adonis. I'll make a profit and get out of my last movie's credit card debt.

ADONIS: And you think the money will come from box office returns, do you?

BENNY: No, from my salary. I'll pay myself $200,000 as writer-director-producer.

ADONIS [*muttering*] That's a good scam.

BENNY: Good what?

ADONIS [*optimistic tone*]: It's a good plan. [*Footsteps indicate a small group entering the room.*] Well, here come the suckers and sycophants.

ACTORS shamble in. They are MARCO, the big fat guy; MR. MacKAY, the drama teacher in the yellow suit, and RANDALL, the naïve young go-getter in a wool cap, sweater, and ripped jeans.

MARCO [*huffing and puffing*]: This building needs a ramp.

ADONIS: Marco, you just had to walk up two steps. Is that going to kill you?

MARCO: What if I tripped?

ADONIS: That's a good point. If *you* took a tumble, this whole building would collapse on us.

BENNY: Come on in guys. Sit at the long table. Adonis, have you got the video rolling?

ADONIS: I do. [*To everyone:*] People, I'll tape this reading, so Benny can present it to possible backers of the film.

MacKAY [*suavely*]: It's like the reading of a will.

BENNY: Better than that, Mr. MacKay. It's the reading of the movie script, *M*U*D*.

RANDALL: Is that why your baseball cap says *M*U*D*? We were wondering about that at the coffee shop.

BENNY: Yes, and that's why I'm wearing the cap here.

MacKAY: Wasn't there already a film with that title?

BENNY: This is an acronym, for "Magyars Under Duress."

MacKAY: Tell us more about the movie. I see my name on the script I'll be reading.

BENNY: *M*U*D* is a high concept, action-adventure-horror-comedy-family drama-road movie. I'm going to raise five million dollars from backers.

ADONIS: Why don't you just hold a rummage sale in Beverly Hills? Those idiots throw away twelve hundred dollars on a sweater I can buy here in Seattle for eighty-eight bucks.

MARY DITTMAN enters, pushing a walker. She is a well-dressed, old woman.

RANDALL: Ma'am? Ma'am? Can I help you sit down?

MARY: Thank you, young man. I'll just set my walker next to me.

BENNY: Let's introduce ourselves to the camera.

MacKAY: I'm Mister MacKay, and I was Benny's high school drama mentor, after he moved here from the Bronx.

BENNY: Tell them who you're playing, Mr. MacKay.

MacKAY: Oh. My personalized script says I'm cast as THE KILLER. That sounds promising.

RANDALL: I'm Randall Lord. I work as a barista for Bremerton's Best Coffee. I'm cast as JACK CROWN.

BENNY: Isn't this better than a one dollar tip for a latte?

RANDALL: You bet.

MARY [*creaky voice*]: I'm Mary Dittman. I used to make costumes for plays directed by Adonis North and Mister MacKay. That's how I know Benny Dorian. I'll be reading the role of JILL CROWN.

Marco's chair creaks loudly.

ADONIS: I hope that chair doesn't collapse under Marco's girth.

MARCO [*wheeze*]: I'm Marco Wright. I played the hero's beer swilling roommate in Benny's master's thesis film, *Epiphany in the Frat House*. I'll read the part of JOHNNY CROWN.

BENNY: Let's begin. I know the script so well that I can recite the description: "Fade in. Daytime. Exterior. Clouds whirl around in the sky. Helicopter shot shows JACK CROWN, lying face up in a field. Zoom in on him, as raindrops splatter onto his face. Jack is blatantly dead."

RANDALL: You killed me before I had any lines!

The other actors chuckle.

BENNY: All right, all right. Refocus, people. [*Back in storyteller mode:*] "Lightning arcs around a white Corvette. Rain pours down, shattering a rainbow and with it, hope."

MacKAY [*as THE KILLER*]: "Moo-hoo-hoo-ha-ha! I win again."

BENNY: "The clouds part and a golden ray from the sun shines down on the Corvette's driver's side door. JILL CROWN steps out. She's the genius mathematician kick boxer. She wears a jogging bra and short shorts, which display her sleek body. Jill is my fantasy."

MARY [*reading JILL in her creaky voice*]: "You killed my brother!"

BENNY: "Jill pulls an Uzi out of her purse. Click-clack. Lock and load. She leaps up, sprays THE KILLER with gunfire. Thwack, thwack, thwack! Bullets riddle his torso. He falls down dead. Or is he? Jill does a combat roll on the ground. She jumps up, runs to Jack."

MARY [*as JILL*]: "Jack! Jack! Oh, why? Damn it, why?"

BENNY: "Jill spies a crumpled piece of paper in Jack's cold, dead hand. She tries to take it, but his death grip is too tight. Focus on her face. With just one look, she conveys that this important clue will solve everything. Her eyes show the horror of what she must do. She breaks his fingers: crack, crack, crack!"

MARY [*as JILL*]: "That hurt me more than it hurt you."

BENNY: "The note says, 'We are the immortal super-Lapps, guardians of the Northern Lights of Sweden. We will halt the neo-Nazi takeover of Uppsala University's physics department.'"

RANDALL: Shouldn't I have read that line?

BENNY: "Rustling noise. Jill looks up. The killer is alive! He lunges toward her. Jill riddles him with more bullets, this time hitting him squarely in the face. Kabuki! His head explodes into gray powder. The killer falls down, this time actually dead. His right hand twitches. Jill shoots it off. Jill stands amid the carnage. The audience can virtually smell the cordite. A child's voice comes from the Corvette." [*Pause. Out of storyteller mode:*] That's your line, Marco.

MARCO [*bad imitation of a child's voice*]: "Mommy, when do we get ice cream?"

MacKAY [*interrupting*]: Hold it. I have one measly line.

BENNY: It was important. You establish mood for the rest of the picture.

ADONIS: What part am I going to read?

BENNY: You're here for running the video camera, picking up pizza, and moral support.

MARY: Excuse me, but you refer to the super-Lapps.

BENNY: That's right.

MARY: They don't want to be called Lapps any more.

BENNY: They don't? What do you call them?

ADONIS: Little weirdoes up north!

MARY: No, they want to be called the Sami. I'm shocked at you, Adonis.

RANDALL: Maybe he can make that joke because he's part Sami.

ADONIS: No, I can tell that joke because I'm a bigot.

MacKAY: I beg your pardon, Benny, but I have a question. I'm an avid collector of pistols, shotguns, and rifles. Are you familiar with the use of firearms?

BENNY: Not the actual shooting of them. I learned all this from reading screenplay writing books.

ADONIS: What a shocking revelation.

MacKAY: Do you think someone's going to give you five million dollars to back this picture?

BENNY: Why wouldn't they, Mr. MacKay? It's high concept.

MacKAY: It's at the same concept level as cage fighting movies. How come so few of us are here?

BENNY: That's part of the high concept. Most of the film deals with the mother and son's character arc as they drive cross-country, shooting at bad guys, and dodging subpoenas from family court. This picture will generate a lot of money.

MacKAY: It's already a big hit [*melodramatic pause*], at the gas station. You made me drive twenty miles to get here. I could have literally phoned in my performance. Am I going to appear in this movie?

BENNY: Well, I've already got commitments from name actors. I will need someone to drive the catering truck.

MacKAY: Catering truck?

BENNY: Everyone on the set will adore you, because you bring them the staff of life.

MacKAY: This is a joke, right? I mean, you're just hazing your old teacher, aren't you?

BENNY: Let me explain it to you [*back in storyteller mode*]: Fade in. Daytime. Exterior. You leave your house to behold the golden sunrise and purple clouds that skirt along the Cascade mountains. You'll drive the truck to bring box lunches to the actors on set. They'll smile upon you. You will lovingly prepare their dinner and dessert. You'll wash dishes, then journey back home when traffic is at its lightest.

MacKAY: That's well after dark.

BENNY: It'll be a great way for you to make contacts.

ADONIS: Sure. Eventually, the actors will let you take their kids to MacDonald's.

MacKAY: I don't need to make contacts to be a hash-slinger or glorified babysitter. I'm a professional actor.

BENNY: But you're not a name-actor. My leading lady starred in a network TV show that ran for a full season in the 1990s.

MacKAY: Is this your idea of paying me back for all that encouragement in high school?

BENNY: I need your help on this, Mr. MacKay. I'd really appreciate it.

MacKAY: I have a better idea than catering. I'll serve as technical advisor about firearms.

BENNY: That's all right, Mr. MacKay. I've learned enough from watching action movies.

MacKAY: No, I'm a teacher. Let me start your education in the subject right now. Here's a piece from my collection of revolvers.

Mr. MacKay pulls a thirty-eight caliber pistol and fires.

BENNY: Stop it! I hate violence!

Benny runs out. More gunshots follow.

MARY: Run, Benny!

MARCO: Wait a minute! [*Pause*] Did he say something about pizza?

MacKAY: I'll win again.

MARY: Don't kill him, Mr. MacKay.

Mary hurls her walker, which decks Mr. MacKay.

MacKAY: Wow! Mary's walker knocked me right off my feet.

RANDALL: She saved Benny's life.

MacKAY: I'm not trying to kill him. I'm trying to shoot that stupid baseball cap off his head. [*Fires again.*] Damn! I keep missing. [*Click, click*] Benny, stop! I need to reload.

ADONIS: I'm glad we're videotaping.

RANDALL: Yeah, you can't write stuff this good.

ADONIS: Sure, I can. Benny can't.

CURTAIN

Bob's Progress

I turned off the alarm clock just before it could ring. My normal routine started, culminating in me emerging in the bedroom, in a Navy blue pinstripe suit and orange tie. I paused at the dresser, where a document awaited. I folded it in half, then in thirds, so that the single sheet of paper fit into my shirt's front pocket.

I'd forgo my usual cornflakes and eat at a diner this morning, after taking care of business at work. My job was to sell men's clothing at a Thomas A. Bank store. I grabbed my twenty-five-year-old Volkswagen Rabbit keys. Contentment and confidence filled me, as a I glided into the garage.

Then I halted like a speeding garbage truck at a red light. The place was empty.

I rushed back into the house and found my brother, reading the *Seattle Times* at the kitchen table. He sits in his wheelchair all day long, and telecommutes.

I asked, "Hey, Tim, where's the car?"

"Mom took it. She has to drive back over the mountains to Spokane."

"And she took our wheels? She's just visiting us."

Our mother had come by train to Seattle.

Tim said, "You didn't let me finish, Bob. I gave her permission."

"Why?"

"Brace yourself. Grandma had a stroke and fell into a coma. They moved her to a hospice."

I collapsed into a vinyl kitchen chair. I looked to the framed picture of our grandmother, a jolly, solidly built lady with lush white hair, and sprightly eyes twinkling out of large, square framed glasses.

"Why am I so shocked?" I asked, "Grandma is ninety-seven."

"That doesn't make it any easier on Mom."

"Or us. I've got to call the store. We have a buy-one-get-one free sale on suits."

I stood up and glanced at the credenza. My cell phone charger was empty. I looked toward the garage, but remembered having left my mobile phone in the VW. Curses! That made me grit my teeth, and snap my fingers in a downward motion.

I walked over to the landline and picked up the receiver. No dial tone came to my ears. I hung up and tried again.

"The phone company was supposed to fix that yesterday afternoon," said Tim.

"Everything bad happens at once. I'll see you later."

I walked out the front door, and automatically touched my shirt pocket. This ritual arose from a fear that the document might have slithered out on its own. It bent against my left pectoral, reassuringly.

I walked several blocks, grimacing with each step. Black dress shoes were not made for long-distance walking. The right shoe rubbed against the back of my heel. The left shoe abraded my big toe. I anticipated corns and blisters.

Payphones aren't as common as they used to be, even here in Ballard, a Scandinavian suburb in Seattle. I dug two quarters out of my pocket and dialed the store. I reached one of my co-workers, but had to shout over buses and trucks trundling by: "This is Bob Draugensen. Can you tell Rex I'm going to be late?" I explained the reason, then asked, "Did you get that? Thanks. Goodbye."

I hung up and trudged to the bus stop.

When the bus did pull up, all seats were full, and I gripped a post for the whole ride. The vehicle bounced along the roads and took many sharp turns, making me feel like a wool-clad surfer. Someone on board gave off a putrid potato smell from unwashed clothes and inadequate bathing practices.

I hopped off the overcrowded bus a half mile from my work place, and thanked the driver.

The trek began on Stewart Street, where I unintentionally made eye contact with a bearded man in dingy jeans and sweatshirt, two sizes too large for him. The teary eyed man clasped his hands together and entreated,

"Sir? Sir? Can you help me, sir? My house burned down. A candle fell over, after our power was cut off. My wife and I are living in a homeless shelter. That's her over there."

He pointed vaguely to a large crowd at a bus stop on the next block.

He continued: "A church will give us a place to stay, if we come up with twenty dollars. If you can spare anything, I'd really appreciate it. Anything at all. God bless you."

I pulled out a quarter and offered it to him.

"That's it?" he asked. "Hang onto that quarter, sir. You need it more than I do."

He hung his head and shuffled away. I shouted over the din of cars driving past us: "I remember you! You told me the same story five months ago!"

I stood at the intersection, waiting for the light to change, next to a plump girl in a miniskirt. Fishnet stockings made her thighs look twice as large. Long, bleached hair contrasted with black eyebrows. She said to a paunchy man in a silk bowling shirt and polyester golf pants, "Look, honey, you paid for a girlfriend experience. It's $300, and a minimum of $100 just for meeting me."

"You don't look like your picture," he rasped, "I didn't pay your boss for a fat chick."

"Look who's talking."

He attempted to suck in his stomach, then snarled, "You're lucky we're in public."

"I'm not," I interrupted, gratuitously.

Both of them shouted, "Shut up!"

Well, at least I gave them common ground. The light turned green, and I set off through the crosswalk. My own business deal awaited.

A crowd blocked my path in Westlake. It's a courtyard park, with rows of leafy trees, benches, and large square or rectangular granite blocks as interactive art.

A wiry, bald man with a black goatee stood in the middle of a circle of onlookers. He clacked two wooden spoons rhythmically in a windmill motion, then chanted with a big smile:

"I'm a spoon man!
And I'm spooning to eternity.
Won't you come and spoon with me?
Please be my spoon woman.
I will be your spoon man.
Croon, croon, croon with a spoon,
We'll get married soon.
Spoons!"

I weaved my way through the crowd, past the street performer. He stopped his merry doggerel, which made me instinctively look back over my right shoulder. The performer gripped his spoons in tightened fists. He pointed one of his instruments at me and shouted, "Hey! You! Yes, I mean you, the corporate jerk in the suit. Nobody walks out on Artoris the Spooner. This show ain't free. What do you make, a hundred thousand bucks a year?"

Individual faces scowled at me from the crowd.

I announced, "I make minimum wage, plus commission, minus Social Security, Medicare, and Federal Withholding Tax. I hope you contribute to those programs."

I made my way through frowning onlookers. One pulled out a five dollar bill and called out to the street performer, "I'm sorry you went through that, Artoris."

Artoris said, "I'm accustomed to cruelty from lackeys of corporations."

"We love you, Artoris!" shouted a woman. Onlookers applauded. Coins clinked into the courtyard, undoubtedly in support of the emotionally wounded spoon player.

The crowd would forget me. I turned a corner, and it was as if I had traveled twenty miles.

I couldn't help noticing an apple-shaped redhead in a miniskirt and tight blouse, walking ahead of me, southbound. She fiddled with some gizmo, like an Ipod.

A stubble faced man in a baseball cap, smudged, blue windbreaker, and baggy jeans stepped out from a doorway. He watched her, too. The middle-aged bloke matched central casting for a pervert. He ogled the redhead up and down, smirked, and took three steps in her direction.

I quickened my pace until I was parallel with the girl. I met the pervert's leer with a hard glare.

He stopped dead in his tracks. The creep's eyes took on the soft entreaty of a scolded Dachshund. He held his palms out in front of him, and backed away.

The girl kept walking, blissfully unaware, for two more blocks. She turned up another street and headed into a coffee shop. I don't know what I protected her from, probably a groping or theft. God help her next time.

At long last, I walked into the clothing store. I patted my shirt front pocket once more, so that the paper crinkled audibly.

Rex Holden, our blond haired, blued eyed Nordic manager, stood at the counter, while reading receipts.

I clunked along the hardwood floor and said, "Rex, I'm sorry I was late. Did you get my message?"

Rex nodded, but didn't look up.

"It couldn't be helped. My visiting mother took the car, because my grandmother is at death's door in Spokane. My brother stays at home alone in his wheelchair, but he can look after himself."

Rex didn't respond right away. I wondered if he had heard me. Rex said, "I can't believe you guys don't have a car."

Somehow, that response didn't surprise me. I said, "Rex, I need to talk to you about something else."

Rex pulled a sack of garbage from behind the counter and threw it right at my face. I put up my hands automatically and blocked it, so the bag dropped to the floor. My manager grunted, "Take this trash to the loading dock."

"Okay, I'll do it, but first I've got something important to tell you."

"I don't care."

"It won't even take a minute of your time."

"Garbage is a higher priority than anything you could tell me."

"No it isn't."

"Stop your backtalk."

"Rex, this is important."

"Take out that sack, or I'll kick you in yours."

I considered the bag, then met Rex's glare, smiled brightly, and said in the cheeriest of tones, "Oh, shut up."

Rex's head snapped up and his blue eyes bulged. He growled, "Communist! I'd better not have heard that." He stomped around the counter and confronted me. His voice rose to a shriek: "Do you want me to go off on you? Because I will go off on you!"

I pulled the document out of my pocket, unfolded it, and held it in front of Rex. This was a neatly typed termination/resignation form. I announced, "I was going to give two weeks notice. You don't deserve that much courtesy."

Rex smacked it out of my hand, and shouted, "Don't expect a recommendation from me!"

"I don't need it. I landed a position at North Seattle Community College."

"Doing what? Washing trays in the cafeteria with Asian refugees?"

"Teaching freshman level composition. It's the lowest job in the English Department, but a step up from this place. I wish you a happy, serene life."

"I'll get you for that!"

I walked toward the front door.

A youth in jeans and a T-shirt jaywalked from the opposite sidewalk, made a beeline for our shop's door, and opened it. The young man grabbed my arm, and said, "Sir? Sir? Can you help me, sir? I need a black, three button-suit with flat front pants for a wedding tomorrow morning. It's an emergency. I'm the groom."

"I'm sorry, I don't work here."

I glanced at my arm, then back into his pleading eyes. His face became quizzical, until he looked down at his own hands and belatedly released my arm.

I said, "If you look next to that trash bag, you'll find a charming gentleman. He's Rex, the store's Nietzchean Super-manager. I'm sure he'd be overjoyed to help you."

Rex kicked the sack of garbage, then flapped his arms. The young customer backed away, but I said, "It's all right. Just show Rex some compassion. He needs it more than I do."

Independent Study

When you research a patient's delusion, you set out to debunk it. I was a graduate student in the Psych Department, and wanted to launch an independent, interdisciplinary study project about supernatural delusions.

My committee chairman was Tom DeForrest, Ph.D., a young man whose boyish face's raised eyebrows made him look pleasantly astonished. When not tossing hardback books to me, he'd suggest ideas for independent papers.

"Ah-oh, Barry," he exclaimed, "I talked to one of my ethnomusicologist buddies today."

Ethnomusicologist is an academic term for someone who studies folk music.

Tom gave me one of his best goofball smiles, and his nose twitched like a rabbit. You couldn't help but like Tom DeForrest. He turned research from a dreary chore into a fun challenge. I waited, trying not to show my anticipation. Tom continued, "He said they have a graduate student in the Music School who had the weirdest delusion he's ever come across."

Tom explained that the patient had recently left the University Medical Center after having been involuntarily committed for 30 days, and voluntarily hospitalized for two further months.

The month-long commitment surprised me. Committing someone in this day and age requires a court order, after a prosecutor proves to a judge that the patient poses a danger to himself, others, or is gravely disabled.

"The patient's name is Scott Blank, and he studies piano composition."

Tom told me what Scott had done, so I leaped at the chance. It would incorporate abnormal psychology, criminology, and folk tales not related to zombies. At Tom's behest, I contacted the patient's therapist and got permission for an interview, on condition of the subject's anonymity.

A week later, I dashed across the Quad into the Music Building. I raced up the stairs to the graduate students' offices. Number 304G had the patient's name on a printed scrap of paper, inside a transparent name plate.

I rapped on the door three times. An unfamiliar piano concerto emanated through the door. Perhaps Scott Blank didn't hear me, so I rapped again, only louder. His portal creaked open. A curly haired man towered over me. He asked in a deep, mellow voice, "Are you Barrington Dandridge?"

"I am."

"Come in." He extended a long arm, and then his wide palm and lengthy fingers enveloped my hand when he shook it.

The concerto continued. The patient had a piano keyboard in his office, and a desk covered with sheet music paper. One page sat in the middle of the desk. It was half covered with musical notes and symbols, done in pencil.

It had never occurred to me that musical composition contained a visual component, like drawing. Some composers don't read music, let alone write it down.

Scott nodded to a black vinyl chair, and I sat. He turned the CD player down a notch, sat in a swivel chair, and crossed his long legs.

"Thomas DeForrest called me," said Scott, "I assume you're here for some research purpose. My therapist saw nothing wrong with it."

His voice sounded pleasant, although he didn't smile.

"Yes," I replied, "he told me you had suffered from a complicated delusion."

"It's pretty simple, really. The local court didn't commit me for just believing in a vampire outbreak. I had heard it on my car radio, repeated fifteen times: 'All recently deceased corpses will soon reanimate as vampires. Citizens are ordered to take action at once. Use the ancient process known as binding.' Then it explained how to do it. A news anchorman cut in with an announcement from the Oval Office. I heard the President's voice say, 'I urge all Americans to follow the instructions just given. Your lives, the souls of your loved ones, depend upon your swift action.'

"So, I followed the radio's advice. I drove to a funeral home and said I had to get to the nearest service for a friend's Dad. They gave me the location of Saint Jerome's Catholic Church. I stopped at a hardware store along the way."

"In other words," I interpreted, "you acted on the delusion."

"I did more than that."

The patient explained how he marched down the aisle of the church, feeling the eyes of confused mourners upon him. Scott bowed his head respectfully, and held his clasped hands in front of his chest, as if in prayer. He actually held the head of a five pound hammer.

Scott barely heard their sobs and sniffles. The organist stopped playing "The Lost Chord." Everyone watched the young man in the Navy blazer and gray slacks march calmly past them. Scott Blank walked around the coffin and faced the front of the sanctuary.

The deluded composer told them of a radio bulletin, which warned everyone to follow suit because of the vampire epidemic.

And then Scott pulled a wooden garden stake out of his belt, and positioned it on the dearly departed gentleman's breastbone. People in the congregation screamed or sat silently, mouths agape. Scott raised the hammer high.

Fortunately, the priest charged over and decked him with a sucker punch to the left cheek. Several mourners then restrained young Mr. Blank until police arrived.

Thus ended the anecdote. The narrative came across as pat, and well practiced from numerous interrogations and therapy sessions.

And then I imagined how the short, weird tale could inspire a great scholarly paper. I'd pore over newspaper articles, court records, and conduct extensive interviews with witnesses.

II

I asked Scott Blank, "What happened before the radio broadcast?"

"My hallucination about radio messages, and the delusion, didn't come from trauma, overwork, drugs, or a chemical imbalance," he intoned.

Psychotics often have shaky voices from fear; or halting delivery from regret; or a dreamy quality from a state of unreality. Not so with Scott Blank; his baritone resonated, though it lacked emotion.

His pale, blue eyes rarely blinked. He had virtually no facial expressions, and didn't emphasize the tale with gestures. His long forearms rested in his narrow lap.

Furthermore, despite bizarre, well-documented behavior at the funeral, he still seemed benign and detached, rather than cold.

I asked, "Were you under major stress from your studies?"

"No, the stress was more of a social nature."

The patient didn't strike me as the sociable type. Sure, he was reasonably good looking, even if his face was a little on the long side. Women probably admired the short, dark curls on his head.

He dressed too well for a college campus. Students like me walk around in jeans and T-shirts, not sports jackets. He was a study in blue and gray: Navy blazer; powder blue, button-down shirt; blue neck tie with purple medallion design; gray slacks; black shoes. He defied our casual conventions.

I asked, "So, what happened of 'a social nature' which led to your action?"

"The other musicians in the department had been razzing me about how I've never had a girlfriend, never go out on dates," he paused as if something discomforted him, "and never had…" His voice trailed off and he looked down. This was the only break in his delivery.

I put in for him, "…never had physical relations with a woman."

"That's right," he said, and stared back into my eyes, "Drummers and guitarists get all the women. Pianists are background music."

It was not my place to say that his own shyness caused isolation. I asked, "How could they have known this about you in the first place?"

Scott explained that several young men congregated in the Graduate Student Lounge. They had bragged about sex acts in graphic terms, then had noticed that Scott didn't participate in the conversation. They hounded him with probing questions, and realized that he didn't know what they were talking about. They had gathered around him as he sat on a couch, until he admitted he hadn't slept with a woman.

The other musicians had found his weak point. Ridicule and criticism continued.

Scott Blank explained how his colleagues had teased him unmercifully as "The Virgin on the Piano." They treated homosexuals with reverence, womanizers with admiration, but scorned a fellow musical artist for celibacy and dedication to his craft.

He would exit the building on spring days, and find cliques of music students sitting on the steps, chatting or sunning themselves. Several would see him, and say, "Make way for the Sainted Virgin." That would cause the others to laugh at Scott. One tormentor liked to say, "He's saving himself for marriage."

"Just shut your eyes and think of England," another had taunted. Every joke drew loud laughs from his colleagues.

I asked, "How did you react to all this teasing?"

"At first, I tried to explain that musical composition is my real passion."

Passion was not a word to apply to the patient. He continued, "When that didn't work, and they kept teasing me, I would keep walking and ignore them."

None of them every scooted aside for Scott Blank. He had to step around their seated forms, like an escaped POW dodging landmines.

Scott's attempt to ignore them just made the activity more fun for the tormentors, because they got away with it. Harassment continued for six weeks. They finally wore down his impassive façade. He reported their actions to his committee chairman.

"Did your advisor discipline them for their harassment?"

"No."

"Did he put the issue of vampirism into your mind?"

"No, it never came up. He put everything in motion, which led to the curse."

"Curse? Do you mean your illness?"

"No, I mean an actual, literal curse."

"Do you believe there was one?"

"Was and is, Mr. Dandridge. It's real," Scott Blank continued. "My committee chairman said the guys were trying to get me to come out of my shell. He told me to loosen up and become one of the combo. He called their intentions good, because they wanted me to socialize more. Then he gave me the number of an escort service. He said, 'I use them sometimes.' That seemed plausible, since he's a portly, bald man with an inky-black dyed beard. The service had an inviting name, too: 'Hot Coed Escorts.'"

I couldn't picture Scott Blank holding hands with a bimbo, let alone in bed with one. I asked, "Why did you go along with it?"

"Everyone had ganged up on me. I was a laughingstock, and my committee chairman had authority."

And so the curly haired young man made an appointment, hopped into his Volkswagen, and drove to the local University Arms. The escorts were regular customers who paid an hourly rate.

Everything had gone wrong. The hotel room door opened and the girl hid behind it, until Scott Blank entered. She closed it behind him, and stood in her underwear. A protruding belly slopped over her black underpants. She had hips two ax-handles wide, too much greasy makeup on her face, and oily, dyed red hair.

Much to my surprise, Scott changed expressions while relating this part of the story. He winced, forming crows' feet at his squinting eyes' corners.

Scott had told the woman that she wasn't what he expected, and he'd have to leave without paying.

The shabby woman had snarled, "Look, buddy, you'd better pay up, or face some big time consequences."

"You can't sue me for an illegal act," he had told her, "In fact, if you don't stop bothering me, I'll call the police and turn in both of us. I'll do the same if you send loan sharks."

That impressed me. He had taken a stand.

And then the chubby chippy had said to him, "You can't pull that on me, or this company." She announced herself as one of a coven, then insulted him by adding, "You wouldn't be here if you could find a girlfriend, loser."

He responded to her without raising his mellifluous speaking voice, "If I ever need to crush my libido, I'll picture you."

"You owe me for my time and the price of this hotel room!"

"You're not getting any money."

That just made her angrier: "Then I'll curse you."

Scott Blank didn't bother to wait around for the incantation. He simply opened the door and walked away.

Scott had handled a bad situation quite well. So why would that send him into a psychosis?

He said the illness had started with bouts of anxiety, which grew into anger if he jogged or lifted weights. Scott often felt as if a sinister presence watched him through a window. He thought all mirrors were two-way observation devices, with that same eerie force spying on his every move.

Scott found solace in one activity. He could play his new concerto and the anxiety would drain away, clearing his head.

But then early one afternoon, he had driven his Volkswagen en route to a concert hall. Anxiety built up into full scale paranoia, and he scoped out the pedestrians. Something intangible seemed wrong with them, especially the pale ones. They must be part of the sinister, watchful presence.

He had flipped on the radio to his favorite classical music station, but instead hallucinated a news broadcast about the vampire plague, complete with orders from the President of the United States.

We all know the rest.

I sat there stunned. He had a delusion about the onset of the delusion.

I asked, "How did the vampire delusion end? I assume major tranquilizers helped."

"Haldol let me sleep at night. I'd wake up to the same overwhelming sensation of bloodsucking ghouls watching me through the window of the hospital."

"Something else could have contributed to your initial psychotic break. Did you watch a lot of vampire movies?"

"I hadn't even thought about vampires. I live for creation of music that inspires and soothes." He still showed no emotion, even when citing the driving force in his life. "My music will live after me, even if it's just as sound recordings in the Library of Congress."

"So, what happened after what you call 'the curse?'"

"She called it a curse."

"Did you see vampires when you were hospitalized?"

"No. Maybe that's where the Haldol prescription helped. But I still believed in their presence. It continued like this for a month. And then one day, I walked around the hospital and found a piano in the recreation room. I sat down, and played my composition." He nodded toward the CD machine, playing an endless loop of the tune. "And that's when the delusion went away. I realized that there were no vampires, only a spell cast on me by the witch."

"Wait, you still think the curse was real?"

"Yes, I know it was. While I played my composition, I tried an experiment. As soon as I stopped playing, the anxiety returned. I sat and waited. It slowly turned into fear, then outright terror. A breeze blew outside and a branch scraped at the window. I leaped up and thought for sure a vampire tried to break in. Then I sat down and played the composition again. No more fear. I experimented with different songs, classical pieces, improvisation; nothing erased the fear except my concerto."

"Then what did you do?"

"I called for a nurse's aide, and asked her to bring me a tape recorder and blank tape."

"Did she do it at once?"

"No, she had to ask permission from two nurses and three psychiatrists."

I snorted, "Pecking order."

"Right. Eventually, she returned with the tape recorder, and I played for an hour and a half. I have it on tape and play it lightly on ear phones, a mini-cassette player, or in my VW's tape deck. I have it on CD here and in my apartment. It's background music all the time. I don't need to concentrate on it any more, so the notes don't interfere with my newest compositions." He nodded to the sheet music on the desk.

"And do you still think the curse is real?"

I would have expected irritated tones in his voice, but it remained mellow: "Yes. The curse is completely real. I don't feel the need to answer that question again."

"I have one more question. Why did you stay in the hospital for two months after your involuntary commitment ended?"

"Because now I was sane, remembering what I had done in the House of God, in front of a bereaved family and friends. I've never felt such overwhelming guilt before. I would turn on the tape of my concerto, but stare at a blank wall. The witch won."

"How?"

"I hated myself."

"I'm glad you're using the past tense. How did you come out of it?"

"The priest from the funeral."

"The one who knocked you flat on your back?"

"Yes. He came to see me, and I told him the same story I told you. The priest forgave me and said it wasn't my fault. He visited again with a letter signed by the family."

He stood up and put his finger on the frame of a document, mounted on the wall like a diploma. A typewritten letter said:

> "Dear Mr. Blank:
> "We realize that your actions arose from forces beyond your control. We accept your heartfelt apology, and recognize your penitence.
> We forgive you."

Multiple signatures followed at the bottom of the page.

I thanked Scott for his open and honest behavior with me, and wished him a speedy recovery.

I left that office, walking on air—figuratively speaking. This would be better than an independent study paper. We're talking about a dissertation. I'd find it easy to write, like a true crime paperback sold in supermarkets. I couldn't wait to interview the feisty priest and horrified mourners.

I also felt special disdain for the bad influences in his music department. Why hadn't they minded their own business? Perhaps they envied his talent. Scott Blank would enrich the world with his musical gift.

Oh, he had a gift all right. I expected him to play sold out classical concerts, though he lacked the humor of Victor Borge, the past pro football glory of Mike Reid, and gaudy flamboyance of Liberace. Too bad he had the madness of David Helfgott.

I would avoid implications of Scott Blank's committee chairman. Artistic people dote on bohemianism, but his was blatant pandering. The man could lose tenure. Considering the confidentiality of the situation, I would keep mum.

One aspect of the paper excited me. I would call the Hot Coeds—strictly for research purposes.

III

It wasn't hard to find the Hot Coed Escort Service, thanks to their ad in the Yellow Pages. Prostitution remains illicit, but escort services constitute a marginally legal business.

I had never hired a hooker before, and hadn't planned on it. A corpulent, over-the-hill professor, bashful classical pianist, or an adulterer might feel desperate enough to pay for affection, but I didn't. I'd shell out money for an interview.

I had some of my own nervousness. What if this prostitute placed a post-hypnotic suggestion in Scott's mind? That might mean his description of a curse was accurate. Perhaps he was suggestible. That goes hand in hand with creativity.

Here were my more genuine anxieties. One was arrest in a sting operation. Maybe vice cops had taken over the business, to catch clients who paid for the women. Another fear was the Murphy Game. That's where you get robbed by the harlot and, usually, an accomplice.

In order to avoid the likelihood of arrest, I called from a payphone.

A giggly girl voice answered, "Hot Coed Escort Service."

"Hi, I was hoping to set up an appointment."

"That's great, hon," she said in bouncy tones, "What kind of escort were you looking for? Redhead? Blonde? Asian?

"Surprise me."

"Ooh, a risk taker. I like that."

"Will it be you?"

"Sorry, hon, I'm answering phones all day. I'll send Debi. Where would you like to meet? Your place?"

"My friend recommended the University Arms."

A pause ensued. Her voice grew serious: "Who recommended it?"

"A prof in the Music School at the U. The hotel is conveniently located for me."

"Well, then you'll have to pay another fifty dollars."

"That's fine." I gave a time, an alias, and told her I'd rent the room.

"What do you look like, hon?"

"I'm tall, slender, I have straight brown hair, and wear glasses."

My goal was to eventually meet the girl who sparked the delusion. If my escort matched Scott's description of the fat woman, I'd interview her immediately. It didn't matter yet. I wanted to establish trust. If this were a different girl, I'd be okay. I'd ask about the coven mentioned by Scott so that she could laugh it off. Then I'd ask to interview the real woman who had met Scott Blank on that fateful day. This could lead to another interview. Besides, the more sources on my citation list, the better.

This is good research, people. You needn't spend all your time in an archive.

I arrived at the University Arms and rented a room from the manager. He wore a short sleeved white shirt, with a green tie. He had neatly combed hair. The man smiled, showing perfectly white teeth, winked, and said, "How long, buddy? One hour or two?"

"Is there a price difference?"

"Yup." I felt dirty handing him the cash, as the fee for an hour. A picture on his desk, by the phone, showed him with a smiling woman and small girl in a pink dress.

He tossed the key in my direction. I fumbled and it clattered on the linoleum. As I bent down to scoop it up, my host said, "I don't know who you're meeting, but they prefer that room. Have a good time."

I scooped up the key and left the office. My flesh crawled after dealing with this man.

I plodded up the concrete steps to the second floor. The number had nothing ominous about it. I opened up and entered an uninteresting room. Shortly thereafter, someone tapped on the door.

I opened up and found myself facing an attractive blond, with short hair. She wore a modest black and white sundress over her lean figure. The lady had a tattoo on her ankle, but I couldn't make out what it portrayed. She wasn't beautiful, but she was cute. She had sharp features, and twinkling gray eyes. "I'm Debi. Did you call for an escort?"

"Sure, come on in."

She walked in, closed the door, and hugged me. I stepped back and said, "Look, I'll level with you. I'm not an intimate client." Nevertheless, I pulled a wad of twenties out of my pocket. "I'll compensate you for your time."

"Sure, baby," she purred. "That's what you pay for. Affection is strictly for free."

"Is that your defense in court?"

She looked at me askance, "Are you in law enforcement?"

"No, I'm a graduate student."

"Oh, great," she muttered. "I knew you were too good looking for this. What are you? Another sociologist, or are you a cultural anthropologist? You aren't some preachy theology student are you?"

"I'm studying Psych," I replied. She walked past me toward the bathroom. I continued, "I'm doing research on a man who used your service once."

"That narrows it down. Was he married? Single? Fat? Covered with acne?"

"None of the above. In fact, he never hired you."

"Oh, didn't he?"

"No, he hired some voluptuous redhead."

"Voluptuous? You mean fat, in her case. She's lazy about learning new skills. I wish that sloppy skank could change her shape."

The interview showed promise. I said, "Look she had an appointment with a man who backed out on the transaction, never even paid her."

Debi turned around and watched me with her wise, gray eyes, "What happened after he welshed on the deal?"

"Well, bear in mind, he was committed shortly thereafter."

"Oh, she did one of her curses."

"Yes, it was about undead beings."

"She doesn't make men see zombies everywhere. It's too cliché."

That stopped me for a moment. "No, he developed an acute psychosis about persecution by vampires."

"That sounds about right."

"Post-hypnotic suggestion, wasn't it?"

"No," she said in off-hand boredom, "it was a curse."

Debi walked into the bathroom. I followed her. "Look, I'm planning to write a paper about the patient's breakdown."

"Are you going to publish this paper?"

"Well, yes, I'm going to present it at conferences, and publish the dissertation as a book."

"That won't help business if the cops and IRS find out about us."

She checked her blush and lipstick in the three-paneled mirror of a medicine cabinet. Each panel was its own door to the interior shelves. I could see over her head, so she stood around five foot five. Her blonde hair had no dark roots. When she opened the mirrored medicine cabinet, the converging reflections of two panels had an odd effect. It appeared as if she had one eye, instead of two, in the middle of her forehead.

I cringed, stepped back, and retreated down the little hallway to the bedroom suite.

I heard her feet walking after me, "Are you okay, buddy?"

I looked back, and her face appeared normal.

"Sorry," I responded, "I didn't mean to walk out on you like that."

"Is something wrong?"

She passed me, and stood in front of the door.

"Well, it seems silly to mention it."

"Silly? Why?"

"I guess it's the power of suggestion, what with the patient's experience."

"What happened?"

"The mirrors on the medicine cabinet made your face look a little different."

"Oh, really?" Her voice changed to a growl and built into a shout, "Did I resemble a Cyclops?"

Her two gray orbs converged into one glaring, red-veined eye. She shrieked in triumph and grew ten inches before me, and her sundress changed to a black toga. My ears filled with an internal roar caused by tightened neck muscles.

She barred the door, and I didn't want to touch her. The red colored nails on her hands turned into long sharp claws. The sexless creature's voice growled, "Do you want to feel post-hypnotic suggestion?"

I turned and tore the curtains off the window. Iron bars locked me inside.

I tried to run around the clawed Cyclops, but it headed me off every time. It spoke: "Madness isn't enough for you. My talons will silence your voice forever."

I looked at a heavy bookend on a shelf, but the Cyclops picked up the chair at the desk and held it up as a shield. I glanced around the room for another weapon. For some reason, I asked myself silently about the pillow.

The Cyclops cackled, "You can't smother me."

I thought verbally about the hotel room key in my pocket.

"Blinding Polyphemus worked for Odysseus, but not for you."

I thought a question.

The Cyclops replied, "I am the most powerful witch in the coven."

I thought again.

The Cyclops said, "I can hear your thoughts when I am in this form."

It responded to another thought, "I made no mistake just now."

I thought: "You are going to kill me."

"I am going to kill you."

"You'll claw me from my feet to my face."

"I will claw you from your feet to your face."

"You'll catch anything I throw."

"I'll catch anything you throw."

"You'll bar my path."

"I'll bar your path."

"Your claws can't grow any longer, can they?"

That was an unwise, silent question. I watched them extend by another six inches.

I visualized a Gideon Bible in an end table by the hotel bed. The Cyclopean witch did not respond. However, it heard the conclusion I drew: "I cannot see your thoughts, I hear them."

I sought to formulate plans through visualization, even as I thought other questions for the Cyclops, and received the following oral answers through its cracked lips and jagged teeth:

"Running water won't stop me."

"I will destroy you."

"Your corpse will be hideous."

"No one will recognize you."

"It will take days to identify your body."

"I am toying with you."

"I am so powerful you cannot escape."

"Suicide will send you to hell."

"I will triumph."

"I raise my claws now."

"My head explodes."

The roaring stopped in my ears, replaced by the ringing from the explosion. The Cyclops had mockingly repeated my thought aloud and the action had occurred as a result. The Cyclopean head turned into a fast ball of fire and blue smoke. The body collapsed.

I sat on the bed and couldn't take my gaze away from the gray corpse. I shook like an earthquake. I asked myself if the monster's carcass would reconfigure into that of the small prostitute.

It didn't.

What had gone on here? I couldn't tell. My problems hadn't ended yet.

I stepped around the body and opened the door. The pimp manager already had my cash for the hour long stay, but didn't have my name. I had parked a couple blocks away from the University Arms, so no one could trace my car. I dropped the key in front of the hotel room door, and walked off.

Had my observation been real? Was it post-hypnotic suggestion? I stopped at a payphone and called the fire department. I said I had heard an explosion in the room, and they should check it out. I gave a phony name and address, then walked away.

You may have read about the fire department, bomb squad, and homicide detectives. Sixty members of the authorities showed up for the event.

They had it under control.

I drove away, unworried. The coven would not find out my name from the cops, the manager, the media, or the madam on the phone. Even now, I'm writing under a pseudonym.

I later told Tom DeForrest that I needed a different topic for independent study. His charming face grew sad. "Really, Barry? Why not this one?"

"I interviewed Scott Blank, but too many invasion of privacy issues would be involved."

Tom nodded and tossed another tome in my direction.

EPILOGUE

Months passed, uneventfully. The Art Building, across from the Music School, had the best café on campus. Raw drizzle in early November gave me an internal chill, right through my jacket and sweater. I plodded downstairs into the dimly lit basement coffee shop. A hot cup of tea would warm my chest from the inside out.

As soon as I entered the room, I stopped. Something unexpected came into the aromas of chocolate, scones, and coffee. The familiar concerto played. I jostled my way through the crowd of young music lovers all sitting or standing around a corner piano.

There sat my favorite composer, Scott Blank. I couldn't help interrupting his serenade. "Hi, Scott, remember me, Barrington Dandridge?"

Without missing a note, he looked me in the eye and nodded.

I continued: "I decided not to write the paper."

"That's okay," he intoned, over the soothing music.

"By the way, Scott, you were right about that business you mentioned."

"Thanks," he replied, "My committee chairman complained that their number had been disconnected. He's still trying to find them."

I held out my hands on either side of me and asked, "Are these your Music School colleagues?"

"Not the ones I told you about. They graduated and moved on. I like these folks a lot better."

I had to watch carefully, but he smiled briefly.

A young brunette reached up and tapped my shoulder, "Sir, we'd like to hear the composition."

"You're right," I replied. The piano's notes filled me with warmth and peace.

The Saga of Krait Hall

The virtual downfall of the Nordic Studies Department at this university began with office politics. Ellen Westby knew the situation mostly second hand, but never quite caught up.

For her, it started in her second month as a graduate student. She walked along the main hallway on the second floor of Krait Hall. A bloated figure clomped down the wide passage. He had a puffy face the same color as a stop sign, from his jowls all the way to the few blond and gray hairs combed over his balding head. He eased his way down the hall, stumping along with a heavy cane. He rubbed his knuckles on his left hip, where he had suffered a stress fracture some months before. An open tote bag, full of papers, dangled from that hand.

Ellen greeted Prof. Sven Stenhodet in her usual ebullient manner and asked, "Would you like me to carry your bag, Sven?"

"Certainly," he said in his resonant Danish accent, "It looks good for a man of my age to have a little vixen carry his burden for him."

They walked down the hall and nearly bumped into a middle aged blonde Valkyrie. Hallgerd Gunnarsen taught Norwegian history, literature, upper division language classes, and seminars. Her heavy lidded blue eyes looked Sven up and down, snubbed him, and gazed down at Ellen.

"How compatible: a redheaded girl and a red-faced man. Hello, Ellen, trying to score points?"

Ellen said, "Sven looked like he needed help."

"He can manage."

Sven barked at Hallgerd, "How would you know?"

Hallgerd glanced at Sven, and looked back at Ellen, "He's not even on your committee. You need to know who your friends are."

Hallgerd walked off, lifting her weak chin high in the air. Sven dropped his cane. The oaken clatter made Hallgerd jump, turn around, and fix him a glare. Ellen hefted the heavy cane and handed it back to the aging professor. Hallgerd marched away.

Sven muttered to Ellen, "Never mind her."

They stepped into a doorway and found themselves in a corridor of offices that ran parallel to the main hall.

Ellen helped Sven to his office. Too bad it was right across the corridor from the lair of his nemesis, Hallgerd.

"Thank you, Ellen." He clasped her hand warmly, smiled, and closed the door gently.

Ellen walked back out to the corridor and into the main hallway. There she saw the Department Chairman, Torvald Lingby, promenading down the hall with his hand on a coed's shoulder. He said to the blonde minx, "You wrote the best paper I've read in my Viking Age class. You'll go far. Oh, hi, Ellen."

He introduced the red haired Ellen to the blonde minx, "Freydis Eriksen, this is Ellen Westby. She's a graduate student, teaching second year Norwegian language classes. Are the students learning it?"

"Yes, they're enthusiastic and highly motivated." She began to explain her use of drama as a language teaching method.

Halfway through the monologue, Torvald interrupted without looking at Ellen. "That's wonderful. You'll forgive me, but I need to have a private meeting with this student."

Ellen headed toward the main staircase, and passed a young man on his way up. He wore a white turtleneck under his navy blue sweater, with black, diagonal hash marks; and blue jeans. The dark clothes made his pale face stand out. The young man's short brown hair gave him a Germanic appearance. He did a double take and squinted at her quizzically. Ellen said, "Hello."

He halted, looked over his shoulder, then said, "Oh, you're talking to me. I'm not accustomed to that. You look like someone I used to know."

"Are you a student here?"

"Ph.D. candidate; currently I'm ABD."

"ABD?"

"All But Dissertation."

"I didn't see you at orientation."

"Would your experience have been better, if I had attended?"

"I see your point. I'm Ellen Westby."

"Bjorn Dyrhagen. It's nice to meet you, Ellen, but I need to look in on Sven Stenhodet."

"Perfect timing. He's in his office now."

Bjorn cantered up the stairs.

Ellen didn't think much more about Bjorn, since he was reasonably pleasant and non-threatening. The enmity between Sven and Hallgerd gave her an unsafe feeling.

II

A week passed. Ellen gathered all the graduate students, and some of the faculty to watch an open air presentation by her students, on a warm Indian summer afternoon.

Sven leaned on his cane, and clung to the brick wall of the Gothic structure, Krait Hall. Torvald's eyes surveyed the figures of nubile maidens. The little blonde minx, Freydis Eriksen, remained beside him, like any teacher's pet. Hallgerd stood on top of the outdoor stairs, her arms folded. The entrance doors were open, so Bjorn watched from the staircase.

Ellen read the Troll scene from Henrik Ibsen's *Peer Gynt*, aloud in Norwegian, while a tape recorder boomed out Edvard Grieg's classical tour de force "In the Hall of the Mountain King." Her fifteen students pantomimed the scene.

The activity exemplified a language teaching method known as Total Physical Response, but it was also a theatre exercise called Uncle Glug.

Chris Roland, the tallest, blondest student, enacted the title role of Ibsen's verse drama. He got into the part by wearing his grandfather's *bunad*, the traditional finery of Norwegians. He had blue breeches and an ornate red waistcoat, making him look very much the rural Norwegian swain. Chris would occasionally look into the audience of Nordic Studies students, make eye contact with the prettiest girls, and hold their gaze. Then he'd smile, nod, and wink at each one, individually.

Chris tried that routine on Freydis Eriksen. Torvald stood in front of her, blocking the flirtatious student's view. Chris caught Torvald's icy glare, and looked away.

When the elaborate activity ended, each student narrated a half-page, newly written composition, parodying Norse myths and folktales they had read in class. Their fellow second-year Norwegian language students would then mime them out.

The fifty minute session passed in what seemed like five minutes. The faculty applauded and the students bowed.

Sven placed the cane in the crook of his arm and clapped. Hallgerd clapped a few times, in a slow, perfunctory way, then folded her arms again. Torvald applauded with great enthusiasm.

Tom Woods, the folklorist, stepped through the crowd and joined Ellen in the courtyard. "Thank you for that spontaneous outpouring. I'm Ellen's committee chairman, so I assume you're applauding for me."

Ellen laughed as did everyone else, except Hallgerd.

Tom said, "Ellen, we need more creative teaching at this university. Keep it up."

Ellen beamed. It was early in the term, and her students had done her proud.

Hallgerd locked eyes on Chris Roland, and crooked her index finger to entice him closer.

III

The next morning, Ellen sat alone in the graduate student office. She shared it with two other teaching assistants. They were both out.

The Nordic Studies program had two Grad Student Teaching Assistants to lead courses in each modern Scandinavian language: Norwegian, Swedish, and Danish, making for six total. The seven professors divided up their teaching in upper-division Scandinavian language instruction, Graduate seminars, and English language electives about Scandinavian folklore, literature, and history.

Ellen graded papers.

Someone knocked on the door. Ellen opened it and saw one of her top students. "Oh, hello, Chris. What brings you in?" Her voice reverberated with cheer.

"I've got to talk to you," he replied haltingly.

He sat down and looked at her desk. "Look, Ellen, I've really enjoyed learning from you. You make the language and culture of Norway come alive."

"Well, I spent a lot of summers in Oslo. That's where my father came from."

"Yes, and I look forward to your class every day."

"I appreciate that."

He looked up and blurted out in a great hurry, "So, do you want to go to dinner?"

"What?"

"I know a great restaurant nearby."

Ellen couldn't quite figure this out. He had always appeared confident and flirtatious around girls, but his delivery here was tentative, as if recently memorized and not well rehearsed. It seemed like he wanted to get it over with.

"Look, Chris, I'm flattered, but it's not permitted."

"It's okay, if no one finds out."

"I have a boyfriend studying for his MFA in the Theater Department. I don't think he'd approve of this conversation."

"Look, Ellen," he said flatly, "I'm crazy about you."

The lack of emotion creeped her out. She said, "Chris, if this is a distraction for you, then you'll have to sign up for a different instructor, maybe audit the upper division courses. Hallgerd Gunnarsen teaches them in Norwegian. As for a romance with me, the answer has to be no."

"Okay. Forget it." He stood up and rushed out of the room, closing the door behind him.

Ellen analyzed his abrupt, unnatural conversation for a long time. Chris didn't behave like a student with a schoolboy crush. He frequently chatted up girls in the class. His declaration didn't ring true.

Meanwhile, outside, Chris walked down the hallway, his face crimson from embarrassment. Hallgerd stepped out of the shadows. "Well, did Ellen agree to go out with you? Can you get into her apartment?"

"No, she blew me off."

"Are you sure? Was it a mixed message? Did she ask you to wait till the end of the school year?"

"No, she was pretty damn clear. I knew this wouldn't work. Why didn't you tell me why I was doing it?"

"I don't trust that girl. She's too popular with the students and faculty. Ellen also has a perky personality, like a TV weather girl. She grates on me. You sure screwed this up. Maybe I can get Torvald, the Department Chair, interested in her.

"No, you can't do that."

Hallgerd's blue eyes flashed. No one dared contradict her. "And just why not?"

"Professor Lingby has already got a case on some chick in my Viking Age class."

Hallgerd paused thoughtfully. "Oh, really? Tell me more."

IV

Hallgerd's elation over Chris's news turned to euphoria. She barely felt her feet tripping lightly up the stairs, and down the hallway. She picked up some papers in an accordion file in her office, turned out the lights, and locked the door. She placed her jangling keys in the pocket of her raincoat.

She passed Sven wordlessly in the main hall. His stress fracture had to have healed by now. Why was he still hobbling around with that heavy cane? It clunked noisily every time he tapped the floor with it.

She headed for the staircase, then stopped. Something occurred to her. Sven wanted the Department Chair position as much as she did. Both could stand on their records. She could bring her womanhood status into it. But Sven could use his advanced age and perceived disability in his favor.

That's just it. Perceived. He didn't impress her with his act. She turned around, and took off her high heeled shoes. She stuck her hand in her coat pocket to keep the keys from clinking. Hallgerd sneaked slowly through the main hallway, and back toward the corridor of professors' offices. Maybe she could pop in on him at an opportune moment.

Sven's office was right across from hers. A recording of screeching Norwegian Hardanger fiddles assaulted her ears. Why would a Dane suffer through that music?

Hallgerd crept up to the door. She saw light through a crack where he hadn't quite closed it.

She peered through the crack.

The cane lay on the desk. She jockeyed around until she saw Sven in the middle of a Norwegian folkdance. He leaped around with his arms in the air, his back to the door. He bounced from foot to foot, slapped one ankle, then another ankle.

Stress fracture indeed. He had no disability to cite in his application.

A cold breeze hit her cheek and she could have sworn a male voice asked, "What are you doing?"

She stood up straight, and looked around, her eyes bulging from being startled.

No one was in the corridor but her. She had seen enough.

Hallgerd put her shoes back on, and walked out of the hallway. She rubbed her hands together. It just kept getting better.

V

Ellen appeared at Hallgerd's office the next morning.

"You want to see me, Ellen?"

"Yes."

"I'm sorry. I can't serve on your committee."

"That's not why I'm here. You're the undergraduate advisor. I have a concern about one of my students. May I sit down?

Hallgerd nodded. Ellen positioned herself on a chair, posed like an artist's model.

Ellen explained her odd meeting with Chris Roland the evening before. She interpreted the professor's frown as disapprobation over the student's conduct.

Hallgerd actually made mental notes of how that fool, Chris Roland, had bungled the mission. Oh, well, he still had his uses, like the latest plot.

Hallgerd had coordinated her new scheme quite well on short notice. She glanced frequently at her land-line telephone, hoping it would ring. Hope, hope, hope.

And then it rang.

Hallgerd picked up the receiver, "Hello?"

"It's me," said Chris's voice, "Come to the U. Motel."

Hallgerd put down the phone and said to Ellen, "We'll talk later. Lock the door when you leave."

Hallgerd grabbed her coat and dashed out the door.

Ellen sat alone, confused. What was going on?

She got up and locked the door behind her, then walked down the faculty corridor, took a left turn, and strolled into the main hallway.

Footsteps echoed on the stairs. Ellen trotted over and said, "Hi, Bjorn."

"Hello again."

"Have you paid attention to all the goings-on lately?" Ellen asked in her infectiously chipper voice.

"It is a little strange. I saw Hallgerd take off out of here, talking a mile a minute on a cordless phone."

That struck Ellen as odd. Why would Bjorn use that term for a cell phone? Did he refer to email as *the teletype screen*? That was its name in 1942. Allied Naval forces used it at the Battle of Dieppe, France.

Bjorn continued, "I don't like the way she always ignores me." He sighed. After a short pause, Bjorn changed the subject, "You know what, Ellen? You remind me of a girl I once loved. You look a lot like her. Same oval face, same long red hair, same bangs, same arching eyebrows, same green eyes. I just hope you don't behave like her."

"Was she your girlfriend?"

"That's what I had hoped. We dated for a while, and I thought something good would come of it. She'd stood me up two different times, but would always apologize profusely, and say she truly valued my company. One summer night, we were going to see the movie, *Gandhi*, at the Varsity Theater. She showed up an hour late, cleaned out my wallet at dinner, then told me about her new boyfriend."

He related it in a matter-of-fact, anecdotal way, as if time had healed the wound. Ellen said, "That's pretty bad. What did you do?"

"I stopped going out with her."

"Good choice."

"I buried myself in work after that."

Bjorn sat down at the top of the staircase. Ellen joined him, seated several inches away. The recent encounter with Chris Roland had made her gun-shy about showing friendliness toward single men. She tossed in, "I'm going to see my boyfriend tonight."

"That's good," said Bjorn, without interest or surprise. "Is he in this department?"

"No, in theater. I have a B.F.A. in Drama, but I wanted to branch out into different studies."

Now Bjorn cocked his head around and leaned toward her, as if she had said something worth hearing. Ellen explained how she longed to perform in Henrik Ibsen plays on stage in Norway: Nora in *A Doll's House*, the title character of *Hedda Gabler*, Solveig in *Peer Gynt*. Ibsen plays had roles for actresses of all ages, so you were never too old to perform in his masterpieces.

Bjorn asked, "Why don't you portray the abusive wife in *Jeppe on the Hill* by Baron Ludvig Holberg?"

Ellen laughed. That was a classic slapstick comedy from the eighteenth century.

Bjorn added, "You should play one of the female parts in *I Remember Mama* by John Van Druten. It's about a Norwegian family in San Francisco. He based it on a story cycle by Kathryn Forbes, *Mama's Bank Account*."

Bjorn explained how he had embarked on a study of representations of Norwegians in major Hollywood films. He knew the background of real classics, like *The Vikings*, *Commandos Strike at Dawn*, *Our Vines Have Tender Grapes*, *Son of Lassie*, *The Moon is Down*, and the greatest of them all, *I Remember Mama*.

Bjorn opened up when he talked about his area of study, mixing film history with the history of Norway, the immigration experience, and so on. He wanted his dissertation to be as thorough and interdisciplinary as possible.

He planned to devote only a paragraph to drive-in junk like *Viking Queen* and that "relatively recent atrocity", *The Norseman* starring Lee Majors.

"Who's Lee Majors?"

"You really do study hard. He used to play *The Six Million Dollar Man*."

"I never heard of it."

"Well, it's hardly a high priority."

"My whole life is one priority after another right now. I've put teaching highest on the list, but then I've got two seminars, I have to take a German language competency test, and finish a reading list. Then I can start on my thesis."

"I'm glad I finished all of that long ago."

"What bugs me is that we spend so much time discussing theories instead of actual books and plays."

"Exactly. Keep this in mind about Grad School, Ellen. The profs get caught up in theories, like Freudianism, formalism, feminism, naturalism, symbolism, Marxism, and who knows what else. They can't see what's right in front of them. One of my professors said that a critic's job is to look for what's hidden in the text. That's all well and good, but it also teaches Grad Students to ignore the obvious. Can I give you some advice?"

"Something tells me you will."

"You're right. Don't ignore the obvious."

"That's good counsel, Bjorn."

"Thank you."

"There's something else I don't like," said Ellen, "It's the office politics. Some of these professors openly hate each other."

"I know. It makes me wonder how far they'll escalate their behavior." A pregnant pause ensued. Bjorn checked the hands on his wind-up Elgin watch and said, "Look, Ellen, it's been great chatting with you. I've got to get back to my research. Be kind to your boyfriend."

He got up, walked down the stairs, and out of sight.

VI

Hallgerd Gunnarsen dashed up the hill, and along Campus Parkway, leading straight to the motel. The professor waved to her henchman, Chris Roland.

"Are you sure he's in there?" She motioned to the U. Motel, which was half a mile from campus.

"Yes, and he's with that blonde girl I told you about."

"What's her name?"

"Freydis Eriksen."

"Did Torvald see you?"

"No, neither of them did."

"You're such a beanpole, how could they miss you?"

"I'm tall enough so I can look over other people's heads, and watch my target from a safe distance. Besides, Torvald spent most of his time looking down the girl's shirt."

Hallgerd rubbed her hands together and smirked. All she had to do now was wait. "What's their room number?"

"207. So, are we waiting to snap a picture of them when they come out of the door together?"

"No, they could explain it away."

"Then are we going to burst in and take a picture of them in bed together?"

Hallgerd raised her receding chin and tried to look down on Chris, despite the fact that he stood five inches taller than her.

"Chris, you've got a lot to learn. If we take pictures of them looking shocked and scared, then anyone who sees the photos will call us blackmailers."

"Isn't that what we are?"

"No, we're negotiators."

"That's why you're the professor. You're still going to give me a glowing recommendation for Grad School, aren't you?"

"This guarantees it, Chris. I'm just glad you didn't ask me for any sexual favors."

Chris crinkled his mouth in what looked like disgust. Hallgerd didn't notice, since she kept her eyes glued to the door marked "207."

She said, "You're right about one thing. We need to get in there."

"Sure, but how?"

"You leave it to me."

Hallgerd and Chris hatched their scheme, then marched with righteous indignation into the manager's office.

An old man sat behind a desk, while playing solitaire. "Can I help you?"

"Did you rent a room to a tall, middle aged man with curly silver hair and a moustache?"

"Just one? That's half my clientele."

"I mean—" she broke off and turned to Chris, "What time did they come in?"

"Four fifteen."

"Let me check the register." The old man hefted his rotund form out of the chair, shuffled with the energy of a tortoise, plopped into a swivel chair at a desk, and checked a screen. "Yes, I have a Mr. Timothy Landerholm, who registered several minutes before that time."

"Was he alone?" asked Hallgerd.

"Sure, he was alone."

"Did you help him with his bags?"

"Do I look like a bellhop?"

"I'm trying to figure out if he entered the room alone."

"Lady, I don't know. I just rent the rooms. It's all I can do to stay alive on my pension. I don't make that much, and Social Security don't pay the bills, and I need secondary insurance."

"Oh, get me a violin," snapped Hallgerd, "I didn't ask for a sob story. You'll be an accessory to statutory rape if you don't come clean. Your guest has a girl in that room with him."

"Now, how would I know that? And for that matter, how do you know? Are you his wife?"

"I'm the girl's mother."

The old man leaped to his feet, "I'm sorry, lady. How did you know to find them here?"

"This man with me is a private investigator." She nodded toward Chris.

As she spoke, she built up her tone into a fever pitch of rage. "He trailed them from the campus to this motel. Our guest could be committing a crime right now, as we speak. I need to rescue my daughter."

The old man whipped a key off a hook and jogged faster than he had in at least a decade. Hallgerd berated him the whole way, to make him move faster: "You're nothing but a panderer, do you know that?"

"Easy, lady, I didn't know."

"Well, the vice cops will go a lot easier on you if you open that door now. I want to catch that pervert in the act."

"How old is your daughter, lady?"

"She'll be sixteen in three months."

The old man made it halfway up the stairs, until his breathing turned to loud wheezes. He stopped and heaved, desperately trying to catch his breath. He inadvertently blocked the path of Hallgerd and Chris.

Hallgerd reached around the old man's wide torso and whipped the key out of his hand. She and Chris squeezed past the ancient manager, but then slowed their pace.

This was Hallgerd's triumph. Knocking on the door would give fair warning to Torvald Lingby, alias Timothy Landerholm. Now for the big moment. She quietly inserted the key into the lock, then whipped the deadbolt to the left, gripped the knob, and shoved.

Her shoulder thudded resoundingly against the door, because she hadn't unlocked the knob.

The old man wheezed and hobbled over with a pass key. He said between gasps for oxygen, "Guests get a deadbolt key and a knob key."

Hallgerd snatched the pass key and wedged it into the knob. She turned it and pushed her way into the room. Too bad they had lost the element of surprise.

The blankets and flat sheet lay in a heap on the floor. Torvald's trademark blazer, gray slacks, powder blue shirt and club tie remained draped over a chair. Freydis Eriksen's jacket, jeans, shirt, and underwear lay in a heap on the carpet. Neither were in the room.

Chris walked toward a closet, but Hallgerd grabbed his shoulder and pointed toward another door.

Fast running water's soothing noise emanated from the bathroom.

Hallgerd whispered to the old man, "Does the bathroom have a window?"

He shook his head.

Meantime, a handle squeaked and the shower turned to a trickle on porcelain, and then stopped.

Hallgerd put her index finger to her lips. She smiled to the old man and Chris. They listened as the shower curtain's rings clanked against the wall, and plastic sheeting accordioned together. The improvised trio of investigators waited.

The door creaked open.

"After you," said Torvald to Freydis.

Hallgerd felt disappointed that they wore white bath sheets. The minx gasped. Torvald looked up. His blue eyes widened in terror, and his mouth opened into a silent rectangle.

Hallgerd leered. She couldn't help but admire Torvald's glistening pectorals, and abdominal muscles. His wiry arms consisted of ropy sinews. She had never seen him out of a sports jacket before. His physique suggested raw, masculine power, but cringing posture and knitted eyebrows betrayed inward knowledge of defeat.

Seconds passed slowly. Hallgerd didn't mind not having a camera handy. Two independent witnesses in the form of Chris and a hotel manager were enough.

Hallgerd said, "Well, Torvald, how do you explain this?"

Torvald's eyes darted from face to face. "This woman is a licensed massage therapist."

The manager asked, "How's that possible when she's only fifteen?"

Torvald's jaw dropped even farther. He said to the minx, "Freydis, you told me you were twenty."

"I am."

The old man asked Hallgerd, "How old is your daughter?"

"My daughter is fifteen."

The old man pointed at the minx, "But she said she was twenty."

"Oh, well, Chris and I made a mistake. This isn't my daughter; she's someone else."

Chris smirked.

The minx hid behind the open bathroom door.

Torvald blushed deeply.

Hallgerd said, "This looks like a good time for contract negotiations. Torvald, you could lose your tenure. All you need to do is leave your post as Department Chair, and make way for me. It seems pretty reasonable, under the circumstances. I'm not asking much."

"I'll have to think about it."

"Stall all you like, Torvald, but the results will be the same. Come on, boys."

Chris Roland and the motel manager followed three paces behind Hallgerd, with their heads bowed in respect.

VII

Ellen dreaded her daily treks to Krait Hall. Tension had built for days. Even she had noticed stiffness in Torvald's movements on the rare occasions when he stepped outside of his office, and peered around furtively.

Hallgerd had inexplicably stopped speaking to Ellen, either walking past her in silence, or gazing sideways at her before turning around and leaving.

When Ellen pointed it out to Tom Woods, in his office, he said, "Hallgerd only does that to people whom she sees as a threat to her job. I wouldn't worry about it."

"She could make my time here unpleasant," said Ellen.

Tom placed the sides of his hands on his cluttered desk, and steepled his fingers. He said, "Ellen, you're here to get out of here. Grad School is not the real world. Earn your sheepskin with 'Master of Arts' printed on it, and get on with your life."

Tom's little office felt like a safe house for resistance fighters. It emitted a welcoming sensation. Ellen liked the picture of a dragon, drawn by Tom's son. The professor used a heavy, clothes pressing iron as a paperweight for assignments turned in by his folklore students. Ellen thanked Tom for his reassurance, and left safe room into the tense atmosphere of the corridor.

Days passed. Ellen now counted the weeks until she could leave for foreign study. Her only motivation was to come up with action-oriented assignments for students to improve their Norwegian language skills.

Ellen remembered Tom's advice, as she plodded on the brick pathway toward Krait Hall. But then Ellen halted. An ambulance and two police cars sat in front of the main entrance. Her first thought was that Sven must have broken a hip, or suffered a stroke. She ran up the brick stairs to the first floor.

A policeman stood in front of the doors. He said, "I'm sorry, but you can't come in."

"Why not?"

A friendly voice from behind her said, "Ellen, come this way." She saw her advisor, Tom Woods, standing at the base of the outdoor staircase.

She looked inside at the paramedics. The only familiar face was Bjorn Dyrhagen, pointing to what looked like a heap of clothes at the base of the staircase. He gestured in a way that resembled a baseball swing, and shouted to a Sergeant. The Sergeant wore blue rubber gloves, while writing on a notepad. Oddly, none of the uniformed authorities glanced in Bjorn's direction.

"Ellen," Tom repeated, "I need to talk to you." He clenched his jaw and tightened his lips.

Ellen clip-clopped down the brick stairs and joined him. Tom led Ellen to the Quad. The cherry leaves had turned orange and red against the iron-gray sky.

Tom broke the silence: "Hallgerd is dead. One of the undergraduate girls, Freydis Eriksen, discovered the body. I also ran into Chris Roland. He told me that Hallgerd's neck had snapped in such a way that her head rested almost right between her shoulder blades. Let's hope it was a freak accident, and not suicide or murder."

Suicide seemed impossible.

Ellen couldn't conceive of the death coming from murder. Hallgerd's only apparent enemy was Sven, a frail yet fat old man. Hallgerd had needled him, since he literally couldn't fight back.

Ellen remembered that Bjorn didn't like being snubbed by Hallgerd, but he was a gentle soul.

Ellen didn't know about the blackmail of Torvald. Only Chris, Freydis, and a motel manager knew that.

In the days that followed, Torvald and Sven walked with lightness in their steps. Torvald said to Sven, "Say, old buddy, you won't mind if I keep this job a little longer, do you?"

"Oh, of course not, my fine friend." They smiled to each other.

That didn't last long. In the ensuing weeks, Ellen noticed a strong scent of Aquavit on Sven's breath whenever she met him. She wondered if he suffered from the DT's. She passed by his office and heard him shouting, "Stop bothering me! Get out of my office. I said get out! Get away from me! Get away!"

She pounded on the door. Sven opened it. He breathed alcohol fumes in her face. Sweat beaded above his thick blonde eyebrows. His hands shook.

"Are you all right?" Ellen asked.

"Just fine. Just fine."

"Who's in there with you?"

"Nobody."

He closed the door gently.

Nothing made sense to her. Why was she never informed? Why was she always kept on the outside? She felt the way Bjorn complained of being treated. Left out.

VIII

Even when she witnessed an event, Ellen felt left out. One morning, she walked into the Nordic Studies office.

Freydis, the blonde minx, sat in skin tight jeans and a form fitting shirt, on the padded bench. Two men sat on either side of her. Chris wrapped his arm around Freydis's waist, while they snuggled together. So much for being "crazy about" Ellen. A middle aged man in a pinstripe suit sat two feet away from the couple.

Ellen shuffled through the test papers turned in by her students.

Torvald stepped out of his office. Freydis, Chris, and the middle aged man stood up at the same time. The little minx announced, in an impersonal monotone, "Professor Lingby, this is my attorney."

The lawyer stood over six feet tall, with pretty brown hair that brushed the tops of his shoulders. He smiled under a moustache. "Professor Lingby, I'm James Harold Bryant. My client and I would like to see you."

Torvald turned ashen, and swayed. He looked like he might collapse. The Chairman steadied himself on the door and choked out, "Come in."

Chris gallantly escorted Freydis into the office. James Harold Bryant flounced in after the affectionate couple. Torvald locked eyes on Ellen. His face now turned pure white, except for dark circles around his eyes.

He closed the door.

Ellen stood alone, wondering.

IX

Ellen pasted two documents in her scrapbook.

MEMORANDUM TO THE DEPARTMENT

Dear Colleagues:
I've enjoyed my position as Chair for the past three years. It has been a privilege to work with all of you. However, I have recently discovered an opportunity to take a long overdue sabbatical. I intend to study the lives of nineteenth century union organizers in Norway. This is a fascinating subject, which captivates me beyond anything else. Thank you for all of your confidence and support.

Yours truly,
Torvald Lingby

Two days later, an article in the *University Tattler* joined the memo in Ellen's album.

OBITUARY

Nordic Studies Professor Passes Away

The Nordic Studies Department announces another untimely passing. Sven Stenhodet was found in his new office, with his head resting on his forearms, on the desk. He had apparently died while

taking a nap. Stenhodet is survived by two sons.
   This is the second tragedy to befall the Nordic Department in this academic year. Last November, Prof. Hallgerd Gunnarsen died from injuries sustained in a fall down a flight of stairs.

The rest of the article did not mention the three empty bottles of Aquavit in the waste basket next to Sven, nor the many bottles secreted in filing cabinets, his desk drawer, a coat pocket, and behind a potted fern.

X

Two months passed. Ellen's students had performed well on all their tests, original monologues, Ibsen scenes, and oral examinations. She had a restful spring break, and made a fresh start with the new term. Still, she dreaded the bad vibrations of Krait Hall. The passageways looked dark inside, even during clear days.

She checked her mail in the Department Office, then ran into a familiar fellow on the staircase.

"Hello, Bjorn. Where have you been lately?"

"Busy playing detective, as it were."

She assumed he meant his research. Ellen said, "I haven't seen you since the accident."

"What accident?"

"When Hallgerd fell down the stairs and broke her neck."

"No, honey, it was the other way around."

"Do you mean the stairs fell on her?"

"I mean she had her neck broken, and then tumbled down these stairs."

"How do you know?"

"I saw it."

"You did? What happened?"

He looked around, then put his back to the wall.

"What are you doing, Bjorn?"

"I've seen enough movies where the witness gets shot right before revealing the killer's identity."

"Okay, who killed Hallgerd? Don't tell me Tom Woods did it with that antique iron from his desk."

"No, of course not."

"Did Torvald snap her neck with his bare hands?"

"No."

"Wait a minute. Freydis Eriksen found the body. Did she manipulate her boyfriend, Chris Roland, into murdering Hallgerd?"

"Ellen, this isn't a parlor game like Twenty Questions. Sven did it."

"Sven? How?"

"I was at the base of the stairs, and they didn't notice me. That's often the case around here. Sven started by saying to Hallgerd, 'Let's keep this brief. I put a student on hold, on my office telephone. You know I should be the new Chair of this Department. I have seniority, after all, plus a disability.'

"Hallgerd said, 'Sorry, Sven, but you missed your opportunity. I deserve to break through the glass ceiling.' Whatever that is.

"Sven said, 'I'm about to retire to Emeritus status. I need the extra money for my pension. It won't hurt you to wait a year. I also need the medical benefits.'

"She snapped right back, 'You old phony. There's nothing wrong with your hip.'

"'Oh, are you a medical doctor suddenly? I spent two weeks in hospital last spring.'

"'Yes, last spring. You've recovered remarkably well since then. I saw you in your office when the door was cracked open. You don't need that cane. You were rehearsing a folk dance.'

"At first Sven didn't say anything, but then he sputtered, 'That was part of my physical therapy.'

"Hallgerd laughed right in his red face. Oh, she'd caught him all right. Hallgerd said, 'You probably expect to dance with that perky actress who teaches the second year Norwegian language classes. Your whole career is a lie, Sven. Torvald gave me the job.'

"'Why should he?'

"'Because I've got the goods on him. You don't. I found out which one of the slinky coeds he's been meeting at the U. Motel.'

"'Ellen would never do that.'

"'It wasn't Ellen Westby. It was that little bimbo, Freydis Eriksen. Talk about indiscreet. You don't have a chance, Sven. He's got to give me the job, or I'll wreck his marriage, his career, his reputation, and his life in general. You've got to stand aside, or I'll expose your disability ruse. Then you'll be answering to me, because I run this Department.'

"Hallgerd rose to her full height. She must have been close to six feet tall anyway. Then she did a dramatic turn, and marched down the staircase. She stopped right on the landing mezzanine. That's when her eyes lit on me. Her lips parted. It was the first time she'd ever acknowledged my presence.

"Hallgerd didn't see or hear Sven sneaking down behind her, with his cane cocked like a baseball bat.

"I shouted to her, 'Look out!'

"Too late. Sven swung his cane in a horizontal arc, and clocked her in the back of the neck, right at the base of the skull. Her head snapped back, and all the life went out of her. She folded into herself on the landing. Sven moved as fast as lightning, picked her up by her coat collar, and hefted her down the stairs. Then he ran up. He must have had tunnel vision, because he never saw or heard me.

"I ran right after him. I shouted: 'Murderer!'

"Sven rushed into his office, picked up the phone and panted, 'Hello, are you still there? Good, I'm sorry that took so long.'

"It was a good alibi, since records would show him on the telephone. But it wasn't foolproof; the caller would undoubtedly remember being put on hold.

"Then the attendance bell rang, and classes let out. I heard a girl scream, so I hurried back to the murder scene. People downstairs were yelling, dashing back and forth, crying. It was pandemonium. I kept trying to shout over the noise that Sven did it, but no one heard me. I told the cops, who came to investigate, but they tuned me out. Here they had an actual murder, and no one bothered to solve it. I stood right next to the body and yelled my whole story at a police Sergeant. He just calmly took notes, while he looked down at Hallgerd. Not one cop questioned Sven. I was outraged."

Ellen interrupted, "If you were an eyewitness, then why would the police cover up a murder?"

"That would be bad for business. The Department would lose grants. Foreigners and out-of-state applicants would avoid us. Maybe Torvald had a hand in the cover-up, since apparently Hallgerd had a hold on him.

"I didn't let it stop there, Ellen. For weeks, whenever I saw Sven on the staircase, I'd follow along, and call him a hot-blooded killer. I finally broke through his resistance one evening, after dark. He had just walked down to the fateful spot on the landing. I sneaked up behind him and whispered, 'I saw it all, Sven. You killed Hallgerd. You broke her neck.'

"Sven stopped, covered his ears, and shouted, 'Leave me alone!'

"That's when I knew I got through to him. He swilled a lot of Aquavit, whenever I found him alone, probably trying to forget, or drown out my voice. I'd sit across from him in his office. He couldn't tune me out. All that drinking made him irrational. He'd shout things like, 'Stop it! Stop it! You aren't real!'

"I wasn't trying to blackmail Sven, just browbeat him into turning himself in. Well, it's a moot point now."

Bjorn stopped, and let the story sink in. He added, "Look, Ellen, I've got to get back to my revisions. You believe me, don't you?"

Ellen thanked him, and Bjorn walked away. His footsteps echoed down the stairs. She had suspended disbelief throughout the narrative, but now she questioned it to herself. She had definitely seen Bjorn through the door, yelling at the police Sergeant. The latter took notes the whole time. The police must have investigated Bjorn's assertions.

EPILOGUE

Ellen walked down the faculty corridor, stopped, and knocked on the frame of her advisor's open door. Tom looked up from his mass of papers and exclaimed with unabashed cheer, "Hi, Ellen! Come on in."

Ellen entered and perched on the wooden chair.

Tom said, "Did you hear the latest gossip?"

He didn't stop smiling, so she assumed it had nothing to do with

Hallgerd's mysterious death, or Sven's recent demise. Still, she couldn't help asking: "Murder?"

"No, but that's a good guess. Did you hear about Torvald?"

"He's going on sabbatical."

"This is better. He settled his lawsuit."

"Paternity?"

"That's your second good guess. An undergraduate girl named Freydis Eriksen sued him for sexual harassment. She claims he forced her to go to a motel."

Ellen laughed. No wonder Torvald had looked so pale when she last saw him. Freydis and Chris had taken up the blackmail scheme where Hallgerd had left off.

Tom added, "But you missed the best gossip of all. Meet the new Chairman of the Department."

Ellen shook Tom's hand, and congratulated him.

He said, "Thanks, Ellen, but it's not as much fun as you might think. I've got to meet with university lawyers ever other day about lawsuits, and delegate more of the folklore and history courses to Grad Students."

After a thoughtful pause, Ellen said, "Look, Tom, I need to study overseas."

"Again?"

"Yes, I want to do an internship next year at the National Theater in Oslo, as research for my thesis about Henrik Ibsen; and write an independent seminar paper about the current state of the Norwegian film industry."

"Norwegian film industry? That'll take up three pages. Don't forget to start with Henrik Ibsen's grandson, Tancred. He was the country's first major movie director. I do have one other question. What about your boyfriend?"

"He can wangle a way over there, too."

"Why not stay here? Maybe you can file a lawsuit like everyone else. Hallgerd's husband is suing the University for wrongful death. He wants damages based on her projected earnings as Department Chair, adjusted for inflation, over the next thirty years."

"Please, Tom, just get me out of this place. And while I'm in Norway, I'll apply for a Ph.D. program at another university."

"Okay, Ellen, I'll help you get a grant. Here are some good ones."

He rifled through a file cabinet and tossed some stapled papers and pamphlets. Most had logos of Vikings or trolls on them. But one surprised Ellen.

"What's his picture doing here?"

"Oh, that's the Bjorn Dyrhagen Scholarship for practical studies in Norway. I never actually knew him."

"He said no one paid attention to him, and yet he has an endowment in his honor."

"How do you know what he said, Ellen?"

"He told me."

"Oh, I forgot, you're from around here. How did you meet Dyrhagen?"

"I met him here. You must have seen him."

"No, Sven was his committee chairman."

"Right, but Sven died. Who's Bjorn's committee chairman now?"

Tom squinted and pulled his head back in disbelief. He replied, "No one."

"Why not?"

"Come on, Ellen, he died of heart failure twenty-five years ago. I guess with all the current upheaval, no one told you the legend."

"What legend?"

"The one that says he haunts the staircase, where he collapsed and died. It's ridiculous. I've worked here seven years, and I've never seen him."

Ellen mulled over Tom's statement, and her own encounters with Bjorn. She deduced out loud, "Maybe you didn't remind him of anyone."

"Pardon?"

"Nothing."

Ellen picked up the scholarship form. It said, "Bjorn Dyrhagen, 1948-1983."

She commented, "Bjorn said that graduate students are trained to ignore the obvious. And that's just what I did."

Ellen thanked Tom, took the forms, and left the room.

She walked into the main office to collect her mail. Ellen felt an angry presence, and looked toward the closed door of the room usually occupied by the Department Chair. She heard voices.

"Torvald gave me this job, Sven, not you."

"No, he gave it to me, after your fall."

"I know his secrets."

"Oh, come on, Hallgerd. Who doesn't?"

Ellen quietly slipped away, and tiptoed down the shadowy hallway.

She saw Bjorn on the stairs and smiled. He beamed, and the gloom faded from the staircase, replaced by light that eased Ellen's mind.

AFTERWORD

This Afterword comes in place of an introduction. I remember reading Penguin Classics for my college lit. classes. The introductions by obscure professors all had the same theme, "This book is no good." I have waited until the end of this collection, to let you draw that conclusion.

The following post script explains the track record of these stories and their adaptations.

"The Hanger On Drops In" and "Bob's Progress" are the only stories not previously presented to magazine readers or radio listeners. They stood apart from the genres of murder mystery, thriller, fantasy, and slapstick. Perhaps Rolly Harris's survival kept the story out of print until now. I had planned to kill the character, but he became too likeable for such a cruel fate.

"Monty Moudlyn" belongs in the slapstick category. Monty's stories did indeed appear in the pages of such periodicals as *The Ecphorizer* & *A Very Small Magazine*; plus a radio play; and the short movie. You can watch *The Adventures of Monty Moudlyn* on the IMDb website. Monty's Hug Brigade manifesto was a comic routine performed for friends, never published in any newspapers.

After the last Monty Moudlyn publication in 1993, I stopped writing fiction for 20 years. My focus turned to folklore archive research, interviews, freelance journalism, and adaptations of stories as audio dramas.

I first wrote "Lesson Plan" as a short film script in 2012, but realized it would be too expensive for that art form. Rewrites as a short story took no time at all. I've spent many years writing letters to friends and relatives, so I adopted the same approach for composing stories.

Schlock webzine's astute editor, Gavin Chappell, grabbed "Lesson Plan" in 2013.

He later premiered my short stories, "Roscoe Gat", "Independent Study", "The Saga of Krait Hall", and "A Janitor's Territory". The latter appeared in the book, *The Best of Schlock! Fantasy 2013*; and "Lesson Plan" reappeared in *The Best of Schlock! Horror 2013*. Both were printed by Create Space Independent Publishing Platform.

"A Janitor's Territory" had a similar track record to "Monty Moudlyn." Creative writing teacher Bob McAllister had assigned us to concoct a story where reality becomes fantasy. I came up with the unfortunately titled, "Metamorphosis of a Maintenance Man." It stayed in drawers from 1985 to 2013. That's when I glanced through a file of my old writing exercises. This one stood out. I added more detail, scenes, and characters. I also decided to write it concurrently as a radio play and short screenplay.

At the same time, I wrote and produced the audio-drama *My Script is M*U*D*. This slapstick comedy portrayed fantasy becoming reality, serving as a companion piece to the radio version of *A Janitor's Territory*. Both of these voice plays, directed by Kevin Veatch, became finalists for the Parsec Award for Speculative Fiction Podcasts. *My Script is M*U*D* came in second place for the comedy category. You can listen to both shows on www.jasonmarcharris.com.

As stated earlier, I encourage drama students and theatrical troupes to stage *My Script is M*U*D*. They can contact us for permission through this publisher, or via the above website.

Kevin Veatch later directed the 11-minute film version of *A Janitor's Territory*, starring Michael Leonard in the title role. The star's cat, Samba, played the janitor's alter ego. Justin Wayne Lynn won the Best Shorts Competition Award of Merit for Best Supporting Actor, as the smug psychology teacher Mr. Fey.

Some of the stories in this collection arose from nightmares, like three that inspired "Independent Study". The subconscious serves as a great venue for literary research. Adaptations, interviews, and letters are also good ways to hone writing skills.

The foundation of every plot is conflict. I have found that the best way to research conflict is to acquire a highly stressful, low paying job, especially one that relies on direct contact with the public. You'll find inspiration from co-workers and customers.

Thanks for reading the book. I hope we'll meet again.